THE RETURN OF MATTHEW SCOTT

By

KENNETH SPOERL

iUniverse, Inc.
Bloomington

The Return of Matthew Scott

iUniverse books may be ordered through booksellers or by contacting:

*iUniverse
1663 Liberty Drive
Bloomington, IN 47403
www.iuniverse.com
1-800-Authors (1-800-288-4677)*

*ISBN: 978-1-4502-8530-8 (sc)
ISBN: 978-1-4502-8531-5 (ebook)
ISBN: 978-1-4502-8532-2 (dj)*

Printed in the United States of America

iUniverse rev. date: 1/10/2011

Preface

THERE ARE ONE HUNDRED BILLION stars in our galaxy, and billions of galaxies in the universe. It seems more likely than not, that we earth dwellers are not the only living entities in this infinite universe. Throughout time, there have been indications that extraterrestrial beings have visited our planet. There are unexplained ancient specimens such as cave drawings of flying craft and stone sculptures that simply couldn't have been built by man using tools that were available at the time.

The following are just some of many examples:

Etched into a high plateau in Peru's Nazca Dessert, a series of ancient designs stretching more than fifty miles has baffled archaeologists for decades. Along with lines and geometric shapes, they include drawings of animals and humans, some measuring over six hundred feet across. Because of their colossal size, the figures can only be seen from very high above the ground and there is no evidence that the Nazca people, who inhabited the area between 300 B.C. and 600 A.D., were capable of building any type of air craft. Ancient alien theorists surmise that the figures were used to guide spaceships as they came in for a landing, and the lines served as runways.

The Polynesian island of Easter Island is famous for its maoi, the 887 giant statues that are spread along the coast line. Roughly five hundred years old, these monolithic statues stand thirteen feet high and weigh fourteen tons, but some are taller and much heavier. How could human beings, without the aid of sophisticated tools or knowledge of engineering, craft and transport such incredible structures is a mystery to this day. It is believed by some, that it is the work of visiting aliens who left their mark on the island.

Located in the Bolivian highlands, Puma Punku is a field of stone ruins scattered with giant, finely carved blocks. Such precise workmanship on a massive scale would have been nearly impossible without modern tools and machines, and yet the ruins are more than one thousand years old.

During the seventh century, Pacal the Great ruled over the Mayan city of Palenque in what is now southern Mexico. Upon his death, he was buried inside a pyramid called the Temple Of Inscriptions. The intricately carved lid of his sarcophagus has become a classic work of Mayan art, and an oft-cited piece of evidence for ancient alien theorists. They suggest that the carvings show Pacal sitting in a space ship during takeoff. His hands and feet seem to be working some type of control panel, and an oxygen tube is pictured in his mouth.

More recently, and in our own time, numerous astronauts have reported seeing strange things while on space missions. The following examples are taken from published articles:

Major Gordon Cooper, while piloting an F86 sabre jet over West Germany, reported seeing saucer shaped craft that outmaneuvered all American fighter planes before flying off at an unbelievable speed.

Astronauts Ed White and James Mcdivitt, while on a Gemini mission reported seeing a weird metal object with long metal arms protruding from its sides. They took pictures that were never released to the public.

While on the Gemini 7 mission, James Lovell and Frank Borman reported visual contact with a UFO.

Apollo 11 astronauts, Neil Armstrong and Ed "Buzz" Aldrin, while on their moon mission, reported a number of enormous space craft lined up on the edge of a moon crater.

There are many more examples of astronaut sightings and civilian sightings that are available to all who are interested. The internet offers a plethora of information, and I could go on with more examples to support the possible existence of extraterrestrial life, but there is too much to explore for the purpose of this preface.

Finally, I would like to thank the person who inspired the writing of this book. I am the only one that he would tell his story to, and he would like to remain anonymous for reasons the reader is sure to understand after reading this mostly, and I repeat mostly, fictional story.

Chapter 1

MATT OFFERED HIS HAND AS George Armstrong entered the room and the two men exchanged greetings.

"So, how are you Matt?" Armstrong asked.

"Okay I guess, just trying to adjust to life after… It's kinda tough. I just feel like I'm on display and I've got to be careful about everything I say and do"

Armstrong smiled as Matt paused briefly, and then continued.

"I keep getting weird looks from people. It's like everybody looks at me like I'm some kind of nutcase. I don't know, maybe it's just my imagination."

"I think you're probably a bit sensitive to the situation right now. Give it some time. It hasn't been that long," Armstrong said reassuringly.

"Yeah, I guess you're right."

"I was actually surprised to get your call so soon. I figured you'd take more time to let everything sink in."

"So did I, but after the trial, it didn't take me too much time to figure out that I needed to get my story out there. Maybe there's a chance that people won't think I'm crazy if they get the whole story, not just what they read in the newspaper."

"Yeah, I think I understand how you feel. I've got to say, it's a pretty compelling story. For what it's worth, you made a believer out of me.

I'll do my best to present a convincing account of your adventure to the public."

"I'm sure you will George. So where do we start?"

"Let's start at the very beginning. Pretend that I know nothing about your story. I want to hear it from the morning of your disappearance, to the decision of the jury. Whenever you're ready Matt," Armstrong said as he removed a pen and note pad from his brief case and placed a voice recorder on the table.

Matt leaned back in his chair and tried to get in a comfortable position as he began to recount the details of his extraordinary life changing ordeal.

"Okay George, here goes. I think it actually all started the night before. I thought that I was probably just dreaming but, well here's what happened…"

Chapter 2

THE EARLY MORNING SUN CAST its rays through the kitchen window where Amy's five year old son, Jason, sat at the table waiting for his breakfast. The aroma of bacon and eggs drifted into the bedroom where her husband, Matt, was getting ready for work. He sluggishly made his way to the kitchen table. Amy poured a cup of coffee as she observed him grimace while easing himself onto a chair.

"Are you in a lot of pain today Honey?" she asked.

He straightened up as best he could and nodded yes in response to her question.

"Yeah, I didn't sleep very well last night. I kept tossing and turning. Just couldn't get comfortable."

"I thought so. I heard you get out of bed in the middle of the night."

"I got up to take a pain pill. I don't know if I was still half asleep, or dreaming, or what, but I was standing at the kitchen sink, staring out the window and I saw something really weird."

"What's that?" Amy asked.

"There was a full moon last night. I was looking out the window while I was drinking a glass of water, and all of a sudden this huge shadowy object passed by and completely blocked it out. I tried to get closer to the window to get a better look, but it passed by so fast. Then it just disappeared."

"Probably just clouds, or your imagination," Amy responded.

"Yeah, I guess, but I could swear I saw like, navigation lights or some type of lighting on it."

"Maybe you just saw some stars through the clouds."

"You're probably right. Like I said, I was half asleep. Anyway the pills helped. At least I got back to sleep. Don't feel very good today though."

Matt, at only 38 years of age, had premature deterioration of the disks in his lower back. This condition put pressure on the sciatic nerve and at times he would suffer excruciating pain. Simple tasks such as rising from a sitting position or walking could be very difficult for him.

"I'm leaving work early today to meet with Dr. Rayford. He's going to go over the results of my latest MRI and discuss the surgical options."

Noticing the painful expression on Matt's face Amy responded with a concerned tone in her voice.

"I just hope that you listen and take his advice this time. Every time you see him, he tells you that you need surgery and you just brush him off."

"Yeah, I know. I just hate the thought of getting cut open. There's no guarantee that it's going to work you know."

"Well, you need to do something. It seems like your pain gets worse from day to day. I hate to see you like this."

"I know," Matt said as he braced himself against the table and gingerly rose to his feet. He gulped down the rest of his coffee, then leaned over, kissed Amy, and patted Jason on the head.

"I've gotta run," he said as he put an egg and some bacon between two pieces of toast. "I'll eat this on the way. I should be home early today. Got an early meeting at the office, then my appointment at one o'clock. I know the routine. He's gonna show the X-rays to me and try to convince me to let him schedule the surgery. He'll probably be surprised when I finally agree to have it done." Matt Paused and looked back at Amy before walking out the door. "Do you need me to stop for anything on the way home?"

"Yeah, I almost forgot that I was going to take your bonus check to the bank. Can you do that, and will you pick up a loaf of bread? My car is making those strange noises again and I'm afraid to drive it anywhere."

"Sure," Matt said as he picked up his brief case, kissed Amy goodbye, and limped out to his car.

Matt's daily commute from his house in suburban Creekview to the Willis/Cooper advertising agency in downtown Chicago routinely took about 30 minutes. Usually he would spend that time bouncing ideas around in his head as to how he would deal with clients that he would be in contact with throughout the day. Today however, there would be no sales calls. He would attend a meeting to hopefully close a deal with a new client, and then leave the office for an appointment with his doctor. All he could think about on the drive in to work was the course of action that he knew his doctor was going to recommend. Stories of failed back surgeries and the fact that there was no guarantee that the procedure would be successful, made him apprehensive of getting the operation that he had been putting off for months. The severity of the pain that he suffered had intensified lately, and along with the limited mobility it caused him, was enough to convince Matt to accept his doctor's advice, roll the dice, and hope for the best.

Matt drove along the rural road leading to the highway; his thoughts thoroughly entrenched on the day's agenda when he was startled as the sun was suddenly blocked out and a shadow was cast over him by an object much like the one he had seemingly imagined the night before. He hit the brakes and as he came to a stop, he rolled down the window and poked his head out to get a better view of the object, but just as suddenly as it appeared, it was gone. The momentary darkness gave way to bright sunshine. He gathered his thoughts as he tried to come up with a rational explanation for what had just happened. He looked for clouds that could have blocked out the sun, but the sky was clear as far as the eye could see. All that he could come up with was that maybe his lack of sleep the past evening had caused him to hallucinate, or that he had actually blacked out for a second or two. He took a deep breath, put the car in gear, and continued on his way.

Matt reached the office of Willis/Cooper and as he exited his car, he spotted his boss, Alan Cooper. Cooper saw Matt and waited for him and the two men entered the building together. Cooper noticed Matt's limp as they passed through the revolving glass doors.

"How's the back today Matt?"

"Not very good; it's got my whole body out of whack. In fact do you see this little spot right here?"

"Yeah," Cooper responded, as Matt drew his attention to his left arm and pointed to his elbow.

"That's the only spot on my body that doesn't hurt."

Cooper laughed, "At the least you've still got your sense of humor. After you get settled in, come to my office and we'll go over a few things for the meeting today."

"I'll get some contracts from my desk and be there in few minutes." He paused, and then quizzically asked Cooper, "Hey Alan, you didn't hear about any strange weather conditions for today, like an eclipse or anything like that did you?"

"No. Why?" Cooper responded.

"Oh, no reason really, I just thought that I saw something kind of strange in the sky on my way in. I'll see you in your office in a few minutes," Matt said as he limped down the hall to his office to collect the documents he would need for the meeting. He returned to Cooper's office and Cooper waved him in. As Matt took a seat Cooper noticed the pained expression on his face.

"Are you sure you want to be at this meeting Matt? You seem to be in a lot of pain."

"I'll be OK, but just a reminder; I'll be leaving to see my doctor right after the meeting is over. By the way, I got my bonus check in the mail. I wanted to thank you for that."

"You've earned it Matt. It's because of you that we were able to land the Forman account. That one brought in a lot of dollars. As far as your doctor appointment goes good luck. I hope he gives you some good news. I need you to get healthy enough to swing a golf club so you can be my partner at the company tournament in a couple of months."

"If I'm going to play golf in a couple of months, those surgeons better be miracle workers."

Cooper's secretary knocked on the door and interrupted the conversation to remind him that the meeting would be starting in a few minutes. She then placed a large bundle of cash piled on top of a silver serving platter on his desk and left the room. Cooper pulled the platter close to him and arranged the money into five separate stacks on the tray.

"$30,000 in cash looks pretty impressive sitting right there in front of you, doesn't it Matt?"

Matt raised his eye brows as he responded.

"It sure does. The pitch we're making today is serving up the cash. I'd say this gets the point across. I gotta tell you Alan, with the physical condition that I'm in right now, I wouldn't mind taking that cash along with the bonus that you gave me and just disappear to some secluded beach in the tropics for a while. Just sit back and take life easy."

Cooper laughed as the two men got up and made their way to the conference room. The meeting started as Cooper and Matt presented the firm's ideas to the prospective clients. The presentation was successful and a contract was signed for Willis/Cooper to handle the account. After the meeting, Matt returned to his office to get his brief case and car keys. On the way out of the building he stopped by Cooper's office to say good bye. He opened the door and leaned in.

"Hey Alan, I'm leaving for the day. Another successful campaign huh."

"That's for sure. I had a good feeling about that one. Now I've got to get this cash in to the bank before I'm tempted to spend it."

Matt glanced at the bundles of cash piled on Cooper's desk.

"Alan, I'm going to stop at the bank on my way to the doctor's office to deposit my bonus check. It's the same bank that has our company account. If you want, I'll deposit the money for you."

"You won't be tempted to run off to that tropical beach with it will you?" Cooper asked jokingly. "But yeah, I'd appreciate it. I'm kind of busy here."

Cooper gathered up the cash and handed it to Matt. Matt put the money in his briefcase and looked back at Cooper as he exited his office.

"See you in the tropics… I mean tomorrow morning," Matt joked as he walked out the door.

Matt left work and started driving to the doctor's office. He remembered that Amy had asked him to pick up a loaf of bread on the way home. There was a particular type of bread that was sold in an ethnic specialty store near his office. It was the only store that sold the bread that was a staple with the family meals. Matt stopped, bought the bread and continued on his way. He glanced at his watch and noticed that he was running late and would not have time to stop at the bank before his appointment. Rather than be late, he decided to make his deposits after leaving the doctor's office.

He arrived at the medical building and entered Dr. Rayford's office. A receptionist directed him to an exam room where a few minutes later the doctor joined him there.

"Hi Matt, how are you doing today?"

"Well doc I've been better. The back pain seems to be worse than ever. It travels through my hips, down to my legs, and the pills aren't helping as much as they used to. I can't even walk straight anymore. It looks like I've had one too many cocktails the way I hobble around."

"That doesn't surprise me Matt. The results of your MRI show the deterioration in your disks has worsened dramatically since I saw you last."

"I'm only 38 years old and I feel like an old man. I'm even starting to look old with my receding hairline and this bald spot on the top of my head. Even the hair that I do have is turning gray. Of course my wife is nice enough to tell me that the gray makes me look more distinguished."

Dr. Rayford laughed as he leaned back in his chair and opened a manila folder that contained Matt's file and x-rays.

"Well there's not much that I can do about your hair, but your back is another matter. I know that you're tired of hearing this, but I strongly suggest that you consider the surgery that we had discussed months ago. I'll be honest with you, there are no guarantees, but I feel confident that the procedure will at least alleviate your pain, as well as help you to move around more freely. I'm not saying that you'll be able to go out and run around like a kid again, but I think you'll notice some significant improvement."

"Sounds like I don't have too many options Doc."

"Yeah, well if you elect not to have the surgery, I'm almost certain that before too long you're going to need a cane for assistance when walking. As your condition deteriorates even more, it's entirely possible that you'll end up being confined to a wheel chair. I hate to give you these gloomy scenarios Matt, but that's just how serious your condition is, and it's only going to get worse with time."

"Okay Doc you can stop trying to convince me. I've decided to have the surgery. I figure no matter how successful it is or isn't, I can't be any worse off than I am now. Can we get this scheduled as soon as possible, before I chicken out and change my mind?"

"I'll work on scheduling it right away." Dr. Rayford said as he rose from his chair.

"Oh, one other thing Doc; I've got this mole on my neck and I keep nicking it when I shave. Is it anything to be concerned about?"

Dr. Rayford leaned over and examined Matt's neck.

"Let me see. No, these things commonly pop up on people as they age. It's nothing to worry about but I can remove it for you if you'd like. It'll only take a few seconds and it will heal within a couple of weeks. There won't be any sign of it ever being there once the scar heals."

Dr. Rayford performed the quick procedure and told Matt that he would contact him as soon as the surgery could be scheduled.

Matt left the doctor's office. As he drove toward the highway leading home his thoughts were consumed with feelings of fear and anticipation regarding the upcoming surgery. He was relieved that he had finally made a decision, but the fact that there were no guarantees of success weighed heavy on his mind. He reached out to turn on the radio, hoping the music would take his mind off of the operation, and out of the corner of his eye he saw his brief case lying on the passenger seat. He realized that he had been so absorbed in thought of the surgery that he had forgotten to deposit his check and the company's funds in the bank. He was already near the highway exit to the rural road that led home, so he decided to continue on and deposit the money at the local branch of the bank near his home. Matt turned off the highway and as he drove down with the desolate country road, the bright sunny sky turned dark, as if a storm was rolling in. It happened suddenly; not unusual for a summer thunder storm, although he had never seen one approach this fast. He turned his head lights on. They immediately started to flicker and then died out as the engine stalled. The engine failure caused the loss of the power steering. Matt held the steering wheel tight and managed to coast to the side of the road, grazing a guard rail as the car came to an abrupt stop. He leaned forward, clutching the steering wheel as he peered through the windshield. He expected to hear thunder and see lightning, but instead everything was perfectly still outside the car. Then just as sudden as the darkness fell, a blinding light enveloped his car. The car began to shake violently. It felt as though he was resting on railroad tracks and a train was bearing down on him. The chaotic moment passed before he could react to it and the sensation of gently floating on air replaced the violent movements that he had experienced seconds earlier. His vision was completely impaired now by the overwhelming light. A warm tranquil feeling came over him and as the bright lights dimmed, he drifted off to an unconscious state.

Chapter 3

MATT'S EYES OPENED SLOWLY AS he regained consciousness. He was lying flat on his back, seemingly hovering in mid air above the surface with no visible means of support. The surrounding area was hazy as if he was in a dense fog. His body was limp and he could only muster up enough strength to slowly move his head from side to side. There were two bodies in close proximity, also suspended in mid air. He could make out the features of a man and a woman and beyond them; too far away to determine the sex or any distinguishing features, he could see an infinite line of bodies also floating in mid air. He scanned the surroundings and observed that the area was devoid of any material objects. There were no walls, floors or ceilings. It was as if he and the others were levitating in space, entirely empty of matter, much like a vacuum, with the exception that there was breathable air.

Matt closed his eyes and tried to think of a logical explanation for his predicament. His first thought was that he must be dreaming. It would explain the surreal environment and the bodies floating in air.

Memories of where he was prior to waking up in his current surroundings were starting to filter into his brain. He recalled the car stalling on the road as the sky went dark, and the bright light that enveloped him before he lost consciousness. Could he have been in a fatal crash? If so, maybe this wasn't a dream, maybe this was the afterlife?

He opened his eyes and out of the haze appeared two beings. They were human like in appearance, standing about five feet tall. They had slim bodies and a grayish hue to their pale complexions. Their faces were devoid of any human features except for two dark blue eyes. They seemed to be communicating telepathically, exchanging intermittent glances, as they maneuvered effortlessly around Matt's hovering body. Matt felt no threat from the strange beings. They exuded an air of serenity that made him comfortable in their presence. He began to feel drowsy and fell into a state of rem sleep where his brain was caught between consciousness and unconsciousness, leaving him immobile, yet aware of his surroundings. One of the beings scanned his body from head to toe with a device that emitted a laser like beam of light. He felt a slight tingling sensation, and then numbness as the amber colored beam passed over his body. He began to fade from his semi-conscious state. He could keep his eyes open only long enough to see the strange beings disappear in the heavy mist as he drifted off to an unconscious state.

Chapter 4

Matt awoke and raised his hands to shield his eyes from the bright sunshine. He was sitting in his car, resting against the guard rail that kept him from sliding off the road. It was the same spot where he had coasted to a stop after the engine stalled during what he believed to be a sudden thunder storm. He began to collect his thoughts as his eyes adjusted to the light.

"Wow, I must have fallen asleep at the wheel," he said to himself. Matt determined that he must have been unconscious for quite a while because the sun was shining and the pavement was dry. There was no sign of the storm that had moved in so suddenly.

He started the car, adjusted his seat belt, and glanced at the rear view mirror as he pulled onto the road. The car stopped abruptly as he hit the brake and did a double take at the image in the mirror. He raised his hand to his head and ran it through his hair. To his astonishment, there was no gray color, no receding hairline and no bald spot. His head was covered with thick dark brown hair." What the hell," he said out loud, stunned by the reflection in the mirror. He gathered his composure and began to realize that the growth and color of his hair weren't the only strange changes to his body. The constant throbbing pain in his back was gone. Matt opened the car door and carefully eased himself out of the car. The twisting body movement needed to enter or exit the car was always a strain on his back. To his surprise, he felt nothing as he stood upright from his seated position. He began to move gingerly around the outside of the car. With each step, he moved quicker until he progressed to a running pace. He stopped and put his hands on his knees as he bent over to catch his breath. It had been over two years since he had been physically able to run because of his disabling back condition. The severe pain that traveled from his back down into his legs making it difficult to walk, much less run, was gone.

Matt walked back to his car as he tried to make sense of the sudden metamorphosis that had changed his physical being. He leaned on the car and thought back to the moments before he passed out. He recalled that the sky turned dark suddenly, and he remembered the bright light that seemed to swallow him up and transfer him to the hazy surroundings where he met two peculiar beings. It came to mind that they performed some type of procedure or experiment on him. He recalled the amber colored beam of light that emitted from a device that they used to scan his entire body, and it was then that he became free of the pain in his back and legs.

A chill passed through his body and he realized that his experience was not a dream. "Oh my God… they were real," he said to himself. He had heard claims of people being abducted by aliens and dismissed them as hoaxes or wild stories told by delusional people whose mental stability was questionable. His heart was racing as he came to the realization that extraterrestrial beings might really exist, and he may have experienced an alien encounter.

Matt opened the car door and slumped down into the seat. He was emotionally drained and took a few minutes to try and clear his head. Instinctively, he put his key in the ignition and started the car. The sound of the engine snapped him out of his funk, and the first thought that came to his mind was, "How long have I been gone?" He checked his watch and saw that it was 3:00 PM Saturday, June 21. That meant it had been about 24 hours since he left the doctor's office on Friday afternoon. "Amy must be worried sick," he thought as he reached for his cell phone. He frantically dialed his home phone number and after a few rings he was connected to a recording informing him that the number he dialed had been disconnected. Thinking that in his haste, he dialed the wrong number, he called again and received the same message. "This is crazy," he thought. "I know my own phone number!" Thinking that there must be a problem with his phone service, he tossed the cell phone onto the passenger seat. Anxious to get home to his wife, and knowing how worried she must be, he put the car in gear and stepped on the accelerator. The car lunged forward as he hurried home.

Chapter 5

MATT PULLED INTO HIS DRIVEWAY. He exited the car and as he jogged toward the house, he noticed an unfamiliar car also parked there. He looked around for Amy's car but didn't see it. As he swiftly moved toward the large white two story ranch house, he noticed a sign posted in the middle of the front lawn. As he got closer, he saw that it was for a realtor's open house. He supposed that some of the neighborhood kids must have put it there as a prank and continued toward the house, not giving the sign a second thought. Matt quickly scaled the front stairs. His only concern at the moment was to let Amy know that he was safe.

"Amy, I'm home," he called out as he rushed through the front door. As he stopped to wait for a response, he looked around the room and noticed that most of the furniture was gone. He called Amy's name again. A woman holding a cell phone to her ear entered the room.

"I'm sorry, I was on the phone. I didn't hear you come in. I'm Janice Moore. I'll grab a brochure for you and show you around."

"Wait. What do you mean, show me around? This is my house. Where's my wife? Where's Amy?"

Janice was startled by Matt's distraught demeanor as she responded to his questions.

"Sir, I'm Janice Moore. I'm Amy Scott's realtor. This house belongs to her."

"I know that this house belongs to Amy Scott. I'm her husband. Where is she?"

Janice backed away from Matt. She was stunned to hear him claim to be Amy's husband since, as far as she knew, Amy was a single mother. The delusional expression on Matt's face caused her to feel threatened by his presence. She turned and swiftly moved to the front door with her cell phone in hand. "I'm calling the police," she yelled back as she hurried out the door.

"What the hell is going on," Matt thought as he watched her leave. He walked into the kitchen, called out to Amy and impatiently waited for a response. He looked around, and just as it had been in the living room, the kitchen was also devoid of many familiar items. The large wooden table that occupied space in the center of the room was missing. A small card table and four folding chairs stood in its place. Appliances that always sat on the counter top were gone except for a coffee maker and a few Styrofoam cups.

The card table was covered with brochures, realtor's business cards, and a newspaper. The newspaper caught Matt's eye as he shuffled through the pile of documents spread across the table. A caption on the top of the paper read Saturday, June 21, 2010 - first day of summer. He picked up the paper and examined it closer. "Must be a misprint, it's 2009," he said out loud.

Matt's head was spinning as he tried to make sense of the strange goings on. He began to piece together the events that had taken place since his encounter with the mysterious alien beings. How could Amy have put the house up for sale and moved almost all of their possessions out in the short time that he had been gone? How could he have recovered from whatever procedure that the aliens had performed on him in only 24 hours? He looked at his watch, then back at the newspaper. His watch displayed only the time and date leading him to believe that his alien encounter had taken twenty four hours. The newspaper presented another possibility. If the date on the paper was correct, then he would have been gone for approximately one year. His knees buckled and a chill passed through his body as he collapsed onto one of the folding chairs.

Matt slowly regained his composure and tried to recall other clues that might substantiate the time that he had been gone. "The bread," he said out loud, recalling that he had bought a loaf of bread before his abduction. He rushed out to his car and retrieved the loaf of bread. The expiration date on the package revealed that, as did the date on the newspaper the bread was nearly one year old.

Matt felt a lump in his throat as he walked back toward the house. The realization that he had been gone for a year was beginning to sink in. He took notice that Janice Moore was sitting in her car and walked toward her. As he approached the car, she rolled up the windows and locked the doors. "I've called the police," she shrieked through the window. "They'll be here any second."

"Please, just tell me how to reach my wife," Matt pleaded. Janice, fearing for her safety, started the car and began to drive away.

Frustrated and confused, Matt frantically ran back into the house, hoping to find something, a note or document that would reveal Amy's whereabouts. He hurried into the kitchen and tossed the loaf of bread on the table. As he rifled through the documents that were spread over the card table, he was interrupted by a voice calling from outside the house. He walked to the front door and stepped out onto the porch. A police squad car was parked in the driveway with its lights flashing. An officer stood alongside Janice Moore waiting for Matt to exit the house. Janice pointed in Matt's direction. Her voice carried a very nervous tone as she identified him to the officer.

"That's the man who burst into the house claiming to live here, but I've never seen him before."

The officer cautiously approached Matt and requested that he produce a driver's license or some kind of document that would prove his identity. Matt took his driver's license out of his wallet and handed it to the officer. He examined the license, handed it back to Matt and turned to Janice.

"Everything checks out miss. According to his identification, he is Matthew Scott and this is his residence."

"But my client, Mrs. Scott, told me that there was no Mr. Scott. I've had this house on the market for two months and I've never seen this man!"

"I can explain," Matt said, "I've been gone..."

Matt stopped himself in mid-sentence. He realized how crazy it would sound if he continued to try and explain his whereabouts. "Please just tell me where my wife is. I just need to see her," was all he could say.

The officer began to get suspicious. Things didn't add up. Even though Matt's identification showed the house to be his residence, it appeared that he didn't actually live there. He considered divorce as a possibility and Matt might be the estranged husband. There could have been a court order that forbade Matt access to the house. That would explain why Janice Moore would not have known who he was.

The officer instructed Matt to follow him to his squad car and wait there while he called headquarters to check on Matt's situation. Matt stood by the car, frantically trying to come up with a way to explain himself. A few minutes past and the officer emerged from his car. He instructed Matt to turn and put his hands behind his back as he slipped a pair of handcuffs on to his wrists.

"What's going on?" Matt cried out. "You checked my identification. You know this is my house!"

"Mr. Scott, there's a warrant out for your arrest. I'm going to have to take you down to the county jail. You have the right to remain silent. Anything you say, can and will be held against you in a court of law."

The officer finished reading Matt's rights to him, and then put him in the back seat of the squad car. Janice Moore walked over to the officer as she dialed her cell phone.

"I've been trying to reach Mrs. Scott. What should I tell her?"

"Tell her that Mr. Scott is in police custody. He'll be held at the county jail on 10 north State Street."

The officer entered is car and escorted Matt off to jail. Janice watched the police cruiser pull away as she hit the redial button on her cell phone. This time she made contact with Amy.

"Hello, Mrs. Scott. It's Janice Moore. I'm at your house. I don't know quite how to tell you this, but there was a man here claiming to be your husband. He said his name is Matthew Scott."

The phone went silent. Amy was stunned to hear Matt's name.

"Mrs. Scott," Janice said, as she waited for Amy to respond.

"Yes," she said as she recovered from the initial shock. "My husband's name is Matt, or was Matt. He disappeared over a year ago."

"Mrs. Scott, this man produced a driver's license identifying himself as Matthew Scott. When he told me that this was his house I became frightened and called the police. They came and arrested him. They said there was a warrant out for his arrest. I'm sorry, but all I know other than that, is they took him to county jail on 10 North State St."

Amy, still shaken by the mention of Matt's name, nervously questioned Janice. "What did the man look like?"

"He was tall. He had dark hair. That's all I remember. He ran in and out of the house so fast that I didn't get a good look at him."

"That doesn't sound like my husband. He was tall but his hair was gray and he was physically impaired. He definitely couldn't have moved around like the man you're describing to me. Thank you," Amy said as she put the phone down. It was difficult for her to consider the fact that the man who Janice Moore described could actually be Matt.

The authorities had two theories about Matt's disappearance. One being that, he met with foul play and was murdered; his body was disposed of and never found. The other was that he simply took off and deserted his family. The latter was a theory that Amy could not accept. They had a very happy marriage and Matt adored his young son.

She began to surmise that the man, who identified himself to Janice Moore as Matthew Scott, may have been involved in his disappearance.

If he stole Matt's identification, it would be possible that he assumed Matt's identity. She wondered if this man showed up at her home knowing that there would only be a realtor there for the open house. Perhaps he thought he could convince the unsuspecting realtor that he was Matthew Scott, owner of the house. Maybe he believed that he could loot the house of whatever he wanted, and then vanish without a trace. The thought of this man posing as her husband and preying on her vulnerability infuriated her. She grabbed her car keys and left for the county jail. She hoped to face this man and get answers that would give her the closure that she needed to move on with her life.

Chapter 6

MY ARRIVED AT THE COUNTY courthouse. She entered the building, approached the desk sergeant, and told him that she was there to identify the man who was claiming to be Matthew Scott. The officer informed her that the man had just gone through processing and had been apprised of the pending charges against him. A guard appeared to escort her to the cell where Matt was being held.

She approached the jail cell. A man sitting on a bench behind the cell bars came into view. He looked up, rose to his feet, and hurriedly moved to the cell door. Amy stopped abruptly. A feeling of shock and disbelief came over her. Chills rushed through her body as she realized that it was Matt on the other side of the cell bars. Matt wrapped his hands around the bars and called out to Amy in an excited tone. "Amy, thank God you're here!"

"Matt," was all she could get past her quivering lips as her heart began to beat profusely.

"Amy, I can't imagine what you must be thinking right now," he said as it came to mind that to her, and in reality, he had been missing for about a year. To him it still seemed as though only twenty four hours had passed since his disappearance.

"Amy so much has happened to me. Wait till you hear."

Amy began to gain her composure as the initial shock of Matt's presence passed. She moved closer to the cell bars. Tears were streaming down her cheeks as she responded to Matt.

"Where have you been?" She paused. "I didn't know if you were dead or alive."

Matt reached through the cell bars to Amy. She pulled away as she wiped the tears from her eyes. Emotions of heartbreak and anger came over her simultaneously as she began to consider the fact that Matt may have actually abandoned her and Jason

"Matt, you've been gone for over a year. How could you run out on me and Jason like that? Why? Where have you been for all that time?"

"Amy, promise me that you'll hear me out before I start to explain. What I'm going to tell you is hard to believe. I almost didn't believe it myself at first, but now I know that what I'm about to tell you is true."

"Go on," she said tentatively.

"Amy I was abducted." Matt paused as he pondered the best way to begin his story.

"What do you mean abducted? Are you trying to tell me that you were kidnapped?"

"In a way," He looked down toward the floor then back at Amy. He ran his hand through his hair as he thought about how to continue. "That's it," he thought. His hair; He took a couple of steps back and motioned for Amy to look toward his head.

"Amy, look at me."

Amy had been so flustered up to this point that she didn't even notice that Matt's appearance had changed.

"You dyed your hair... You had some kind of re-growth treatments. What?"

"Amy I didn't have anything done. It just happened, and you won't believe what I'm going to show you next."

Matt hopped up on to the bench in his cell, and then jumped off. He landed on the floor and proceeded to do a somersault. He followed that with a hand stand, lowered himself to the floor, and then sprung to his feet.

"Amy when was the last time you saw me move like that? Just as mysteriously as my hair grew back, my back problems are gone."

Amy was at a loss for words. The last time she had seen Matt, he could barely walk. Now he was moving around with the agility of a gymnast. His startling physical appearance and dexterity however, did not provide an explanation for his disappearance. Amy became more perplexed as she pressed Matt for answers.

"I don't understand. I thought that you said you were abducted. Did you go somewhere to get your back operated on? Did you have a hair transplant? What does all this have to do with you deserting your family?"

"Amy, I'm trying to build up to that. If I just come out and say it, I'm afraid you'll laugh... or cry. Maybe you'll just think that I'm crazy."

Her voice was shaky and her lips quivered as she responded, "believe me, I won't laugh."

"Okay. I was on my way home..."

Matt proceeded to tell Amy about the trip home from the doctor's office. He described the sudden storm, or at the least what he had perceived to be a storm. Knowing how preposterous his story was going to sound to Amy, he took a deep breath before continuing on to the abduction. Matt described the aliens and the hazy environment of what he deduced to be the inside of the UFO. He recounted the sensations of floating on air while the aliens observed him and the serene feeling that he experienced while in their presence. He told her how the whole experience had seemed to consume only minutes, but when he woke up in his car he came to realize, or so he thought, that it had actually been about 24 hours. "At that point I rushed home to see you," he said.

"When I walked into the house the realtor was there. She said that you were a single mother and there was no Mr. Scott. I looked around and most of our furniture was gone. I felt like I was in the middle of a bad nightmare. Then I noticed the date on the newspaper. At first I thought that it was a misprint, but as I started to piece things together, I realized how long I had really been gone. Amy I know all this sounds crazy. I hear myself explaining it to you and I can't imagine what you must be thinking. I swear to God, unless I'm totally out of my mind, I'm telling you the truth."

Matt paused as he waited with nervous anticipation for Amy to respond. Amy wanted to believe him even though his story seemed so bizarre, but she couldn't help feeling that he may have betrayed her.

"Matt I want to believe you. I look in your eyes and I feel like you're telling me the truth, but you appear out of nowhere with this fantastic story of aliens and UFOs... I don't know what to think."

Matt pressed his face against the cell bars as he made a vow to Amy. "I don't know how, but I'm going to find a way to prove that what I've told you is true."

"Jason!" Matt blurted out. His mind being in a state of disarray, he had totally forgotten about his six year old son.

"My God, I can't believe that I haven't thought about him till just now. Where is he?"

"He's at my sister's house. We've been living with her for the past six months. I had to go back to work after you disappeared, so she offered to take care of him during the day."

"What have you told him? Does he think I'm... dead?"

"He doesn't know what to think. I told him that you had to go away, but after you were gone for so long I had to explain to him that you probably were never coming home. You don't know how difficult it is to tell a six year old boy that he's never going to see his father again."

Tears gushed from Amy's eyes once again. Matt sensed the mental anguish that she had been through as he tried to console her. "Amy we'll be together again, you, me and Jason."

"I don't know Matt. This has all been so weird. I don't know what to believe, what to tell Jason. I'm sorry, but I've got to go. I'll come back after I have had some time to think about all this."

Matt could only watch as Amy turned and walked out of the room. Although he had to watch her walk away, deep down he knew that getting her to listen to his story was the best that he could have hoped for. After all, he had unexplainably disappeared from her life over a year ago, only to return with an explanation for his whereabouts, that even to him, was difficult to accept.

The jail guard escorted Amy to another area of the court house where she was informed that a police impound wrecker would be at the house to seize Matt's company car and place it in legal custody. In all the confusion she had forgotten that Matt was in possession of a company vehicle. Amy told the officer that she was on her way to the house and she would hand over the keys when they arrived.

Chapter 7

MY ENTERED THE DRIVEWAY AND parked next to Matt's company car. She began to walk toward the house when she noticed that the driver's side door of the car was wide open. She assumed that Matt was in such a hurry to get into the house, that he exited the car and carelessly left the door open. She glanced inside as she closed the door and noticed that the glove box was open and papers were strewn around the inside of the car. The mess seemed strange to her because Matt was always so meticulous about how neat and clean he kept the interior of the car.

As she began to walk toward the house, a police car and tow truck pulled into the driveway. An officer approached Amy and asked for the car keys. She went into the house to search for the keys and found them on the kitchen counter top alongside a loaf of bread. Amy emerged from the house, handed the keys over to the officer, and watched as the tow truck hooked up to Matt's car and drove off.

She walked back into the house and stepped into the kitchen. She took a deep breath and leaned against the counter top as she surveyed the nearly empty room and thought about how lonely she had felt in the house over the past year. She took a cup from the sink and filled it with water. As she sipped from the cup, the loaf of bread on the counter top caught her eye. The variety of bread was a staple in her household until she had been unable to find it in stores. The company that baked this particular type of bread had discontinued producing it six months ago. She picked up the bread and read the expiration date; June 28, - 2009. She opened the bag and to her surprise the bread was still fresh. "How could that be?" she thought. The bread was nearly a year old.

She thought back to her last conversation with Matt. It was the morning of the day that he disappeared. She remembered it vividly because it was the last time they spoke. Amy recalled that she reminded Matt of his appointment with the doctor, and that she asked him to pick up a loaf of bread on his way home. A chill traveled through her body as she thought about the impossibility that the one year old loaf of bread could still be fresh.

Amy recalled earlier in the day when Matt displayed his new found physical prowess as he moved around the inside of the jail cell like an acrobat. She thought back to a year earlier when she accompanied Matt to numerous consultations with a number of surgeons. All said that they would be able to provide him with some relief, but because of his spinal condition, he would certainly have limited mobility for the rest of his life. What procedure could Matt have gone through that would prove all the doctors diagnoses wrong, and who would have performed it she wondered.

Amy began to ponder the events of the morning that she had last seen Matt. She remembered that Matt had risen in the middle of the night, and that he had seen what he had believed to be a strange object blocking out the moonlight as it passed overhead. That morning, when Matt told her what he had seen, she dismissed it as a figment of his imagination or a dream. She wondered now, if it was possibly a premonition, or had he actually seen the alien craft where he would spend the next year of his life.

As unbelievable as Matt's alien encounter story sounded, Amy began to weigh the possibility that it actually happened, considering that there was no logical explanation for his physical condition.

Amy decided to go back to the jail and talk to Matt right away. She didn't know exactly what she believed, or what she was going to say to him, but she knew that she needed more answers for Matt's year long disappearance. She felt that she was owed at least that.

Amy's sister, Kathy, was expecting her to be home soon so she called to let her know that she would be delayed. She dialed the number and after a few rings her sister answered.

"Kathy... Hi."

"Hi Amy; What's up."

Amy paused for a second and then answered nervously. "I've got some news. Are you sitting down?"

"Yeah... what is it?"

"Matt is back... he's home."

There was a short pause, and then Kathy responded with a bewildered tone in her voice.

"What do you mean, he's back?" she replied.

"I can't explain it to you right now, but he's back. He's in jail. It's all really crazy. I'll explain it to you when I get home."

"Amy, what's going on?"

"It's complicated. Don't say anything to Jason. He's going to be confused enough when I try to tell him that his dad is home. I'll be home in a few hours. We'll talk then."

Amy hung the phone up. She felt bad that she didn't give her sister more details but after all, she herself didn't really understand the circumstances regarding Matt's return. Her hands were shaking as she reached for her car keys. She realized that she had no idea of how she was going to react when she got back to the jail. The only thing that she was sure of, was that she was sure of nothing. Matt's story sounded as ridiculous as it did unbelievable, and yet she couldn't disregard what she had seen so far to support his claim.

Chapter 8

THE INCREDIBLE CHANGES THAT AMY had observed in Matt flashed by her mind's eye as she made her way to the courthouse. As outlandish as Matt's story sounded, Amy wanted to accept it as the truth. She didn't know if it was because she wanted so much to believe him, or if it was that she saw no rational explanation for his miraculous metamorphosis.

Amy entered the courthouse and was escorted back to the cell where Matt was being held. Matt rose from his seat and anxiously moved to the cell door when he saw Amy enter the holding area.

"Amy thank God you're back. I don't know what else to say to you, but I swear to God that what I've told you is true. I know that I'm asking a lot for you to believe me."

"Matt, I don't know what to believe. I see the changes in you and I wonder how they are at all possible, knowing what all the doctors have told us. There is something else that's just as strange. When I went back to the house, I saw a loaf of bread on the counter top. The expiration date on the bag was a year old."

"I know. I bought that bread the day that I was abducted. Amy, it is a year old."

"Matt I believe you. They haven't baked that a kind of bread in over six months. The strangest thing is that I opened the bag and the bread was still fresh."

"Amy there's something else that struck me as really weird. When I looked at my watch, I thought that I had been gone for about twenty four hours. I tried to call you. My cell phone was fully charged. I hadn't charged it since the day that I was abducted. That meant it had held a charge for a whole year. I don't know how that could be possible. I realize that you could say I'm lying about the last time it was charged, but Amy I swear that I'm telling the truth."

"Matt, before I came back here, I remembered that you got out of bed in the middle of the night. That morning you told me that you saw some strange object in the sky. Do you remember that?

"Yeah, wow, I'm surprised that you remember. To me it seems like only yesterday but to you…I mean; that was a whole year ago. Something else happened to me that morning on my way to the office."

"What?"

"Just like the night before, a large object seemed to pass overhead. This time instead of blocking out the moon, it completely overshadowed the sun. It lasted for only seconds, and before I could get a better look at it, it was gone. I thought maybe it was just clouds passing by, but when I looked around, the sky was completely clear. Now I'm wondering if my friends from out there were actually watching me the night before and that morning. Maybe they actually had an agenda, and I wasn't just a random selection when the abducted me."

The more that Matt and Amy talked; he realized that the circumstances of his return, as well as of the morning before his abduction, were just as strange as those of his abduction. He tried to recall more of his time on the alien craft, hoping that it would shed some light on his post encounter experiences, but just like a dream fades from memory in the waking hours, he could only remember bits and pieces of the actual abduction.

Their thoughts turned to the task of getting Matt released from jail. He had been booked and informed that his employer, the Willis/Cooper agency, had filed charges of grand theft auto and embezzlement of company funds against him. He would be confined to jail until his arraignment, at which time the Willis/Cooper agency would present a written accusation of the charges against him. He would then post bail and await a preliminary hearing where a judge would determine if the prosecution had enough evidence that a crime was committed, and if so a trial date would be set.

"Amy they're going to keep me in jail until the arraignment. We need to find a lawyer between now and then. I have a feeling that it might be difficult to find one that will represent me when he hears that my defense is that I was abducted by aliens. Hell, even if we get one to take my case, I wouldn't be surprised if the judge skips a trial and sends me straight to the loony bin."

"We'll find one. You'll just have to convince him that it might really have happened, just like you convinced me. Just tell him your story and all we can do is hope for the best."

"That's hoping for a lot," Matt said as he rested his head against the cell bars. For the first time since his return, he began to realize that just because his alien encounter was over, he might not be able to return to the life he knew before it happened. It was a very real possibility that his residence could change from the comfortable house with the white picket fence, to a room behind bars in the state correctional facility.

"Amy we've got to face the fact that I might be spending a lot more time behind bars."

"I don't want to think about that now Matt. I just got you back. That's all that means anything to me right now."

"I'm sorry. I just want to get out of here and be with you and Jason. I want us to be together again." Matt Paused as a thought came to mind. "You know, maybe the worst that could happen, might not be so bad. After all, the company car and all of the money that I was accused of embezzling is going to be returned."

"Matt, where is the money?" Amy asked nervously.

"It's in my briefcase in the car."

A sinking feeling came over Amy as she recalled returning to the house earlier that day. She remembered that the car door was open and the inside of the car was in disarray. Her anxiety was intensified as she remembered that lately there had been a number of home invasions and automobile break-ins in the neighborhood.

"Matt, when I was at the house earlier today, I noticed that the car door was open. I went to close it and I saw papers scattered around the inside of the car and the glove box was open. I didn't see your briefcase."

"You've to get back to the house and search the car for that brief case. Without it I'm not going to be able to explain what happened to the money."

"It's too late Matt. The police came while I was there. They checked the car for any personal items, and then towed it away. I don't think they found a briefcase in the car."

"The car must have been broken into after I was taken into custody. That's why it was torn apart inside. I can't believe what's happening. Things are going from bad to worse. Now I really don't know how we're going to convince a lawyer to take my case. I don't even believe what's happening."

"Matt we'll get through this," Amy said as she reached through the cell bars and held Matt's hand.

"I hope you're right, but what matters more than anything to me is how you and Jason are going to be affected by what happens to me. Have you told him yet... that I'm back?"

"No, I've been trying to think of a way to tell him. I don't feel that it would be a good idea to tell him that you've spent the past year living on a UFO. He's going to be confused enough as it is."

"Yeah, that's for sure, but we've got to find a way. He's going to hear it eventually, and I'd like it to be from us."

A guard entered from outside of the holding area and interrupted Matt and Amy's conversation to inform them that visiting hours were ending for the day. Amy assured Matt that she would search for the services of an attorney and return the following day. They kissed as Matt released hold of Amy's hand and watched as the guard escorted her from the room.

Chapter 9

KATHY WAS ANXIOUSLY WAITING AT home for Amy to arrive and explain Matt's reappearance. She greeted Amy at the door. Amy walked in, picked up Jason and hugged him. Then she gently set him down and gave him a kiss.

"Go to your room and play. I need to talk to Aunt Kathy, okay."

Jason nodded and left the room. Amy and Kathy sat on the couch and Amy told her of Matt's alien encounter. She realized how crazy the story sounded to Kathy as she told her Matt's account of what had taken place. Kathy rose from her seat, took a few steps and turned back to face Amy.

"Sis, does he really expect you to believe that he disappeared for a year because he was abducted by Martians?"

"Aliens Kathy, not Martians."

"Little Green men... whatever! Now he's back and everything is supposed to be normal again. It's just crazy. You can't really believe it."

"At first I didn't, but how do you explain what's happened to him?"

"So he dyed his hair and had a hair transplant. What does that prove?"

"Let's say that's so. What about his physical condition? He could hardly walk before, now he moves around like an athlete. How do you explain that?"

Kathy sat back down next to Amy. She had no answer to Amy's question, but Amy could see the doubt in her eyes. Skepticism was pretty much what Amy expected, although she had hoped for a more open minded response when presented with the details of Matt's story.

"Kathy I know Matt's story sounds too bizarre to believe, but deep down inside I feel that he's telling the truth. Until someone can prove that his abduction didn't really happen, I've got to stand by him."

"I can't tell you that I believe any of what Matt's told you, but you're my sister. You know I'm here for you."

"I know," Amy said as she rose from the couch. Amy took the telephone book from a table next to the phone and began the search for legal representation for Matt. She rifled through the Yellow Pages, not quite sure of what type of lawyer she was looking for. The pages of attorneys seemed endless, listing every specialty from divorce to bankruptcy. Befuddled by the vast array of choices, she sarcastically thought, "What kind of lawyer specializes in alien abduction?" She came to the section listing criminal defense attorneys and was reminded that it was a charge of embezzlement and grand theft that Matt was facing, not whether or not he had an alien encounter. Amy scanned the pages and settled on the firm of Anderson and Finch. She placed a call and made an appointment to meet with the attorney the following day.

Chapter 10

THE NEXT DAY AMY AWOKE, rose from bed and walked to Jason's room to wake him and prepare him for school. She had not yet told him of his father's return, and the dilemma of whether or not to say anything to him at this time weighed heavy on her mind. Amy got Jason dressed and walked into the kitchen where her sister was making breakfast. She sat down at the kitchen table and Kathy poured a cup of coffee for Amy and herself. The two sisters watched Jason eat his cereal as they conversed, carefully avoiding any conversation regarding Matt's return. Jason finished his breakfast and Amy took the last sip of her coffee as she stood up to usher him off to school.

"Go get your books honey; the school bus will be here in a few minutes."

While Jason was out of the room Amy and Kathy had a brief conversation.

"When are you going to tell him?" Kathy asked.

"I haven't decided yet. I don't know what to tell him, or how to tell him. Matt and I'll have to figure it out together."

As Jason walked back into the room, Amy and Kathy quickly changed the conversation to another topic. The sound of the school bus stopping in front of the house prompted Amy to take Jason by the hand and send him off to school. She waved goodbye to her son as the bus pulled away, then walked back into the house. Kathy was still sitting at the kitchen table sipping from her coffee cup as Amy walked in.

"So when is your appointment with the lawyer?" Kathy asked.

"I'm going to meet with him in a couple of hours. I don't even know if he'll take the case. I know Matt's story sounds crazy. I'm just hoping that I can peak his interest when I explain the circumstances to him."

Kathy tried to bite her tongue, not wanting to upset her sister, but she couldn't help trying to prepare her for the worst case scenario.

"I know that you don't want to hear this, but it's very possible, oh what am I saying, it's likely that no one is going to be convinced that Matt's telling the truth. You do understand that, don't you?"

Amy sat still, tightly clutching her now empty coffee cup. She had no response to Kathy's comment or her question. Kathy looked into her sister's eyes and spoke again with a soft tone in her voice.

"I wish you luck sis. You're going to need it."

"I know," Amy said as she rose from her chair. Kathy turned to Amy and reached out to her. They hugged briefly, and then Amy left the room to prepare for her appointment with the lawyer.

Chapter 11

MY ARRIVED AT THE LAW office of Anderson and Finch. She walked through a set of glass doors to an area where she was greeted by a receptionist. The receptionist confirmed her appointment and told her that one of the attorneys would be with her shortly. A nervous feeling came over her as she sat waiting. She was worried that the lawyer would dismiss her as some kind of crazy person. She clung to the hope that he would at least give her the benefit of doubt, and agree to meet with Matt. A few minutes passed and a man came out to the reception area. He walked up to her and introduced himself.

"Mrs. Scott," he said.

"Yes," Amy replied as she rose from her chair.

"Hi Mrs. Scott; I'm Thomas Finch. How are you today?"

"Fine, a little nervous about being here I guess."

"Well, let's see what we can do about that. Step into my office and we'll discuss your reason for being here."

Amy followed him into his office. He pulled out a chair and seated her, then walked to the other side of a large mahogany desk and sat down. He leaned forward and smiled reassuringly.

"So how can I be of assistance to you today?"

"Well," she paused and took a deep breath. "I'm here on behalf of my husband. He disappeared a year ago with a large amount of funds and a car belonging to the company that he worked for. Yesterday he returned with the car and the money in his possession. He went to the house that we lived in before his disappearance to look for me, but I wasn't there. You see, I didn't know where he had been or what happened to him. I didn't know if he ran out on me, or met with some kind of foul play. Anyway, without my husband's income, I didn't have the finances to keep paying the mortgage and all the household bills, so I had to put it up for sale. The real estate company was holding an open house when he arrived. He introduced himself to the realtor, but she was under the impression that I didn't have a husband. You see I had never mentioned him to her, and she was under the impression that I was a single mother, so she became suspicious and called the police. When they arrived, it was discovered that there was a warrant out for his arrest, and the police took him into custody. I was surprised when the realtor called and told me that someone claiming to be my husband had come to the house. I thought that it might have been someone who had stolen my husband's identification. I had always believed that my husband met with foul play and was probably robbed and murdered. The authorities had never found a trace of him through their investigations, and the case went cold. Anyway, I went to the county jail to see who the man in custody was, and I was shocked to find that it actually was my husband."

"From what you've told me, and if I understand you correctly Mrs. Scott, it sounds as if your husband obtained funds from his company illegally, and has now returned to turn himself in."

"Yes, no, I'm not quite sure. He never planned on stealing anything in the first place. He had all the money with him when he returned."

"Well Mrs. Scott, whatever your husband's intentions were, and if he still has the funds in his possession, the fact remains that he had those funds in his possession for the past year. Since those funds did not belong to him and were the property of his employer, just from what you've told me so far, I assume that at the very least he's facing charges of embezzlement."

"Yes," Amy replied.

Finch leaned back in his chair and continued.

" Mrs. Scott it seems like a clear cut case against your husband. You say he admits to taking the company funds. Well, one thing in his favor is that he's returning those funds in full. That in itself does not excuse him, but it may go a long way in obtaining a reduced sentence if he is convicted and incarcerated. Have those funds been turned over to the authorities yet?"

Amy was overtaken by feelings of anxiety as she realized that Matt's defense would be severely weakened with the loss of the briefcase containing the company funds. She gathered her composure as best she could and told Finch that there had been a rash of burglaries in the neighborhood. Amy explained that after Matt was taken into police custody, she returned to the house to find that the car had been broken into and ransacked. She told Finch that when she returned to the county jail to see Matt, he informed her that he left the briefcase containing the missing funds in the car. She didn't see the briefcase and feared that it was stolen when a car was broken into.

Finch could see the increased anxiety in Amy's demeanor as she explained that the funds were missing. He leaned forward and rested his elbows on the desk as he attempted to settle her down by presenting the possibility that the brief case may still be in the car.

"Mrs. Scott, are you positive that the briefcase was not in the car? It may be that you just didn't notice it. After all, as I understand it, you weren't aware that your husband left it there at that point."

"Maybe," Amy replied.

Finch continued. "The police will have the car at the inbound. They'll be searching it as part of their investigation in an effort to recover the missing funds. Hopefully they will have found the briefcase. In the meantime I could look into the reports of thefts and break-ins in the area."

Finch paused as he decided to get Amy's mind off the missing briefcase. He still had many questions to ask her concerning Matt's absence during the past year.

"Mrs. Scott, you haven't yet mentioned Mr. Scott's whereabouts over the past year. Let's talk about that."

Amy looked away, and then looked back at Finch. She had dreaded reaching this point in the conversation. Her lips began to quiver as she searched for the words to begin. Finch sensed her apprehension and tried to put her at ease.

"Take your time Mrs. Scott. Would you like a class of water?"

"No... Thank you."

Finch waited patiently as Amy collected her thoughts. She took a deep breath, and then proceeded to tell him of Matt's abduction.

"Mr. Finch, what I'm going to tell you is very hard to believe, but I beg of you to hear me out."

"Go on," Finch replied.

"My husband told me that he was abducted by aliens."

Amy instinctively expected a negative reaction from Finch. Her voice took a defensive tone as she continued before he had a chance to respond.

"I know that it sounds crazy. I thought so to at first, but there are some mysterious things that have happened to him in the time that he was gone."

She proceeded to tell Finch of the remarkable changes in Matt's physical condition. She explained that he had seen a number of specialists and after second, third and fourth opinions, all had concurred that even with surgery, Matt would have had extremely limited mobility. She told him about the one year old loaf of bread that was still fresh and the cell phone that had held a charge for a whole year. Amy stated her case as best she could and hoped that it was enough to peak Finch's interest and convince him to meet with Matt to discuss his case.

"Mrs. Scott, your husband's story is interesting to say the least. While I'll admit that my curiosity has been aroused by some of the details that you've presented to me, I must tell you outright. This firm does not take on cases that we consider to be frivolous, nor do we take on cases that we feel are not arguable in a court of law. I would have to consider possibilities for your husband's disappearance other than his claim of an alien encounter. Is he fabricating this story of abduction as a defense for illegal activities? Is he mentally unstable, and really believes this outlandish story? Could he possibly be telling the truth? I've got to be honest with you. The latter would be very difficult to prove with the information that you've provided to this point. Without more tangible proof of Mr. Scott's abduction claim, I don't see using it as a defense in court. He may want to consider a plea of guilty. As I told you earlier, if he was to return all of Willis/Cooper's assets, his chances of a lighter sentence would be greatly improved. That being said, I'll meet with your husband, and if I even consider taking this case on, I'll insist that Mr. Scott undergo a physical, as well as a psychological examination. In fact I'm sure that it would be court ordered before any judge would allow such a case go to trial."

"I understand, thank you," Amy said.

Finch and Amy made arrangements to meet at the courthouse the following day. He rose from his chair and escorted her to the reception area. She thanked him again for his time, then left to see Matt.

Amy walked into the holding area of the county jail where Matt eagerly awaited her return. She told him of her meeting with Thomas Finch and that he agreed to meet with Matt the following day. Matt felt relieved that the attorney would allow him the opportunity to state his case even though his story was so bizarre.

Amy told him that Finch made no promises regarding legal representation. Matt asked how Finch reacted when she revealed his claim of an alien encounter. Amy told him that Finch wasn't convinced that there was enough information to use the abduction story in court, and that he may have to consider other possibilities for a defense, including pleading guilty.

Matt understood that convincing Finch, a total stranger, of his abduction was going to be a much more difficult task than it was to persuade Amy, the woman who loved and trusted him. For the time being, he would have to be content in the knowledge that Finch would even present him the opportunity to state his case.

Chapter 12

B ACK AT THE LAW OFFICE of Anderson and Finch, Thomas Finch was preparing for his meeting with Matt. Although very skeptical of Matt's claim of abduction, Finch was intrigued by some of the details of the story that Amy related to him. He decided to do some research in preparation for the meeting by surfing the Internet for information on UFOs and alien abductions. He came across a website for the Thompson Abduction and Research Center. As he studied the site, he became impressed by the credentials of John Thompson, a professor of astronomy, chairman of the astronomy department at state university, and the founder of the research Center.

Finch decided to contact John Thompson to learn more about his organization and get his opinion of Matt's abduction claim. He made a telephone call and was connected to Thompson's office. Finch introduced himself and told Thompson the purpose of his call. Thompson revealed that his organization was comprised of a group of scientists, UFO investigators, and astronauts, dedicated to the continuing examination and analysis of the UFO phenomenon. He informed Finch that his organization seeks out individuals who claim to have witnessed a UFO, as well as those who claim to have had an alien encounter. Thompson explained to Finch that after interviewing these individuals, they would then evaluate and record their claims. Thompson also revealed that astronomers in his organization continually monitored the skies beyond the earth's atmosphere, looking for any kind of movement that would suggest the presence of alien objects. More often than not, movement of objects traveling about the sky, were attributed to space junk or meteors, although on rare occasions, an unexplainable object was detected.

At this point Finch, decided to enlighten Thompson with the details of Matt's abduction claim. He told Thompson that Matt believed that he was gone for only twenty four hours, when in reality, he was missing for a whole year. Finch continued on to tell Thompson of the changes to Matt's physical being. Thompson was noticeably excited as he questioned Finch about the time period that these occurrences had taken place. Finch gave him approximate dates, based on his conversation with Amy. Thompson informed Finch that two other cases, very similar to the one Matt was claiming to have experienced, had come to his attention recently. Both encounters had taken place on or about the same dates as Matt's abduction, one in India, the other in England. In both cases the abductees involved, had disappeared for a year but believed that they were only gone for twenty four hours, and in both cases there had been major health issues that were mysteriously cured. In England, a woman returned cancer free after being told she was terminal and only had months to live. In India a man returned completely healed after a construction accident left him with multiple fractures in his legs, a broken jaw and a severe concussion resulting in a cracked skull. In the man's case x-rays revealed no signs of calcium deposits that would confirm previously broken bones had been healed. The woman was not only cancer free; in fact tests indicated that she never had the disease to begin with.

Thompson informed Finch that in all the years that his organization had been investigating UFOs and cases of alien abduction, they had never come across such compelling evidence to support those claims until now. He told Finch that he would very much like to interview his prospective client. Although still very skeptical, Finch's increasing curiosity prompted him to invite Thompson to accompany him to his meeting with Matt. Thompson eagerly accepted the invitation and they made plans to meet the next day at the county jail. Sensing Finch's skepticism, Thompson decided to enlighten him about a web site that might present him with some persuasive arguments to support the existence of extraterrestrial beings.

"Mr. Finch, I can tell from the sound of your voice that that you're not convinced that Mr. Scott may have actually experienced an alien encounter. I understand your skepticism because I realize that without any evidence to the contrary, these claims are very hard to accept."

"Evidence is the key word. If I'm going to represent Mr. Scott in a court of law, I'll need to prove that his claims are at least possible."

"I'd like to send an e-mail to you. There'll be a link to a web site that I think you'll find very interesting. It contains interviews with some very credible and influential people on the subject of UFOs. I think you'll find it thought provoking at the very least."

"I'd appreciate that. I'll need all the convincing I can get if I decide to take this case. Thanks, I'll see you tomorrow," Finch said as he hung up the phone.

Finch waited for a short time, then checked to see that Thompson's e-mail had arrived. He opened it and clicked on a link that read, "Extraterrestrial Contact - UFO Sightings by Astronauts." The document contained the following descriptions and testimonies given by astronauts Major Gordon Cooper, Ed White, James McDivitt, James Lovell, Frank Borman, Neil Armstrong and Edwin "Buzz" Aldrin.

On May 15, 1963 Major Cooper's Mercury capsule was completing a multiple orbit around the world when on his final orbit; he reported to the tracking station at Muchea (near Perth Australia) that he could see a glowing greenish object approaching his capsule. The UFO was also picked up by Muchea's tracking radar.

The National Broadcast Company was covering the flight, and reported Cooper's sighting, but when Cooper landed, reporters were informed that they would not be allowed to question him about the UFO.

Ten years earlier, while piloting an F-86 Sabrejet over West Germany, Major Cooper had his first UFO sighting. He had seen saucer shaped discs at a considerable altitude that out maneuvered all American fighter planes.

Major Cooper also testified before the United Nations:

"I believe that these extraterrestrial vehicles and their crews are visiting this planet from other planets…Most astronauts were reluctant to discuss UFOs."

According to a taped interview by J.L. Fernando, Major Cooper said:

"For many years I have lived with a secret, in secrecy imposed on all specialists in astronautics. I can now reveal that every day, in the USA, our radar instruments capture objects of form and composition unknown to us. There are thousands of witness reports and a quantity of documents to prove this, but nobody wants to make them public."

"I was furthermore a witness to an extraordinary phenomenon here on this planet earth. It happened a few months ago in Florida. There I saw with my own eyes, a defined area of ground being consumed by flames, with four indentations left by a flying object which had descended in the middle of a field. Beings had left the craft (there were other traces to prove this). They seemed to have studied topography. They had collected soil samples and, eventually, they returned to where they had come from, disappearing at an enormous speed. I happen to know that the authorities did just about everything to keep this incident from the press and TV, in fear of a panicky reaction from the public."

In June, 1965, astronauts Ed White and James McDivitt, while passing over Hawaii on a Gemini mission, reported that they saw a weird looking metal object with long metal arms protruding from its sides. McDivitt took pictures with a cine-camera. Those pictures were never released to the public.

In December, 1965, Gemini 7 astronauts James Lovell and Frank Borman reported visual contact of a UFO during their second orbit of a fourteen day flight. Gemini Control told him that he was seeing the final stage of their own Titan booster rocket. Borman confirmed that he could see the booster rocket, and he could also see something completely different.

The communication between Lovell and Gemini Control went as follows:

Lovell: "Bogey at 10 o'clock high."

Capcom: "This is Houston. Say again 7."

Lovell: "Said we have a bogey at 10 o'clock high."

Capcom: "Gemini 7 is that the booster or is that an actual sighting?"

Lovell: "We have several... actual sightings."

According to former NASA employee, Otto Binder, unnamed radio hams with their own VHF receiving facilities, that bypassed NASA's broadcasting outlets picked up the following partial exchange between Apollo 11 astronauts, Neil Armstrong and Edwin "Buzz" Aldrin:

NASA: "What's there? Mission Control calling Apollo 11..."

Apollo 11: "These babies are huge, Sir! Enormous! Oh my god! You wouldn't believe it! I'm telling you there are other spacecraft out there; lined up on the far side of the crater's edge! They're on the Moon watching us!"

Finch had to admit to himself that, as skeptical as he was on the subject of UFO's, Thompson was right. The accounts given by the astronauts in this document were, at the very least, thought provoking.

In preparation for his meeting with Matt, he continued researching the subject of UFO's. The internet supplied a plethora of information on the subject, some posted by seemingly eccentric individuals or groups, some by recognizably credible people.

Chapter 13

THAT EVENING JASON SAT BY the television playing a computer game while Amy prepared dinner. The early edition of the TV news was on but to Jason and Amy it was only background noise. The news commentators were reporting on the day's events, weather, sports, etc. Near the end of the newscast a commentator closed with what she believed to be a humorous story.

"On the lighter side," she said sarcastically, "a man who had been missing for over a year, claimed that he was abducted by aliens from outer space. Mathew Scott, a resident of suburban Creekview…"

Amy was startled by the news cast and rushed into the room. She promptly turned to another channel, and then looked toward Jason who appeared to be oblivious to the story that was on the television. Amy noticed that Jason's facial expression was unchanged. She hoped that he was so engrossed in his computer game that he didn't notice that his father's name was mentioned.

She turned the television off, walked back into the kitchen, and called for Jason to come to dinner. Jason scampered into the kitchen and hopped onto a chair. Amy slid him close to the table, put some food on his plate, and then sat down next to him. He put a spoonful of potatoes in his mouth, swallowed, then looked toward his mother.

"Mommy, is daddy with Allen?" He asked.

A chill passed through her body as she tried to remain calm. She didn't realize that the news media was already aware of Matt's story. Amy hoped that she would be better prepared to explain Matt's disappearance to Jason than she was at this time. Even more than that, she hoped that Matt and she would be able to do it together. Amy realized now that she would have to do the best she could on her own. She turned toward Jason and took hold of his hand.

"Honey, are you asking me that because of what the lady on TV said?"

Jason looked at his mom with a wide eyed expression on his face and answered her with a very perplexed tone in his voice.

"The lady said daddy's with Allen. Who's Allen mommy?"

Amy realized that Jason didn't understand that the news anchor said aliens, not Allen. She realized that he probably didn't even know what aliens were. Amy felt relieved that she wouldn't have to explain Matt's story to Jason although she knew it was inevitable, and would still be a challenge when the time came. Searching carefully for the right words to say, she answered Jason.

"Honey, daddy had to go away, but he's coming home soon. You'd like that, wouldn't you?"

Jason's young mind was not quite able to comprehend the fact that Matt had been gone for so long, and why he had not come home sooner. He looked up at his mom and answered in a confused tone.

"Yeah Mommy, when's he coming home? He then became anxious as he asked, "Is he coming home today?"

"No honey, but soon. He has some things to do first, but he told me to tell you that he loves you and he'll be home as soon as he can. Does that make you happy?"

"Yeah mommy, then can we go back home?"

"I hope so dear. Mommy and daddy would both like that."

Amy felt that she had told Jason enough for the time being and decided to change the subject. She told him to eat his dinner and then he could watch television until bedtime. Jason finished his dinner and ran into the living room to watch TV as Amy removed the dishes from the table and put them in the dishwasher. She then joined Jason in the other room and collapsed onto a chair next to him. She was mentally exhausted, but somewhat relieved that she made it through the ordeal of telling Jason that his father would be returning home. A couple of hours passed and Amy put Jason to bed. She retired for the night shortly after Jason fell asleep, but she lay awake thinking about the meeting with Thomas Finch and Matt the next morning. Finally exhaustion overcame her and she drifted off to sleep.

The nervous anticipation of the meeting between Thomas Finch and Matt caused a restless night's sleep for Amy. She fell in and out of consciousness throughout the night until the following morning when the alarm clock summoned her to rise and prepare Jason for school.

Amy walked into Jason's room to wake him, and was surprised to find him sitting on the edge of the bed with a baseball mitt in his hand. He sprang from the bed and ran to Amy with all the excitement of a kid on Christmas morning.

"Mommy I wanna show daddy how good I can catch the ball. Is he gonna be home today?"

Amy picked him up and held him close." Maybe, if not today, soon," she said.

Amy got Jason dressed for school and after sending him off on the school bus, she prepared herself for the meeting with Matt and Finch at the county jail.

Chapter 14

MATT ROSE FROM THE BENCH in his cell as he saw Amy enter the holding area. He rested his body against the cold steel bars and as Amy approached the jail cell he reached through the bars to take hold of her hand.

As they waited for Finch's arrival Amy told Matt about the previous evening's newscast and that Jason had learned of Matt's return.

"So he thinks I've been with someone named Allen. I guess aliens would sound like Allen to him. I don't know how we're going to tell him what's really going on. I do know that he's bound to hear it from someone if the story has already made the evening news. I'd rather try to explain it to him before he hears about it from some of the kids at school. I can imagine the teasing he'd be in for. Kids can really be cruel sometimes. I just don't want him to get hurt."

"My God... I sent him to school this morning. It didn't occur to me that the other kids might have heard the news. Maybe I should call the school and have him taken out of class until we get to talk to him together."

"That might be a good idea," Matt replied.

Just then Thomas Finch and John Thompson entered the room. They walked up to the cell and Amy introduced Matt to Finch. Finch introduced John Thompson to Amy and Matt, and informed them that

Thompson was there to listen to, and evaluate Matt's story. Thompson asked Matt to give his account of the abduction in as much detail as he could recall. Matt proceeded to describe his encounter as Finch and Thompson listened attentively. Finch paid close attention to Thompson's reactions, and it became apparent to him that Thompson was impressed by Matt's story. He concluded that, if he were to take Matt on as a client, he would have to be able to present a plausible story in the courtroom. If Matt could present Thompson with enough evidence that his alien encounter may have actually happened, then maybe a jury could be convinced also. Matt finished his story and nervously waited for Finch and Thompson's reactions.

Finch turned to Thompson, "What do you think John?"

"Mr. Scott, I'm very impressed with your account of the abduction. As I explained to Mr. Finch earlier, I've been investigating two other cases that are remarkably similar to yours. There are details of all three cases that mirror one another, such as the date of your abduction and the date that you returned. They also believed, as did you, that only twenty four hours had passed between their abduction and their return. Your physical being is most curious. I understand that before the abduction, you had severely limited mobility because of a degenerative spinal condition, and now you seem to be perfectly healthy."

"Yeah, I could barely get around because of the pain. Now there's no pain and feel like I could run in a marathon."

"In the other cases, one had miraculously recovered from a fatal disease, the other from crippling injuries. When examined by a physician, both had completely healed with no trace of the prior health conditions. I suggest that you contact your physician immediately upon your release from jail and get scheduled for an MRI. I'm very curious to see what the current x-rays of your spinal condition will reveal. If my suspicions are correct, your spine will not only be in perfect alignment, there will also be no evidence to show that a medical procedure was ever performed to correct your physical ailments."

Finch became increasingly optimistic as Thompson continued to reveal how the unexplained details of Matt's abduction paralleled those of the two other encounters under his investigation. Thompson acknowledged, that in all his years of investigating abduction claims and UFO sightings, this was the first time there was ever such compelling evidence to support claims of contact with extraterrestrial beings.

Thompson turned to Finch. "Thomas if you decide to represent Mr. Scott, I would very much like to work with you on this case. What I've learned about Mr. Scott's encounter so far leads me to believe there are more similarities to the other cases that we have not yet uncovered"

Matt looked to Finch, anxiously awaiting his decision.

"Mr. Scott, I must admit that I was very skeptical of your story when Mrs. Scott first came to my office, but it's hard to ignore the things that I've seen and heard to this point. I can't say that I'm completely convinced of your story yet, but the fact that I'm even considering its validity is a good sign for you. I say that, because if I feel that way, then so may a jury. That means there would be a benefit of doubt in your favor when the case goes to trial."

"Does that mean that you'll represent my husband?" Amy asked.

"This is definitely the strangest case that I've ever considered taking on, but from what I've heard today, and what I've read in documents provided to me by Mr. Thompson, my eyes have been opened to the possibility that your story has merit. So, yes I will."

Matt let out a sigh of relief as he thanked Finch. It was comforting to know that Finch believed his story was convincing enough to take to trial.

"Where do we go from here?" Matt asked.

"There will be an arraignment within the next couple of days. You'll enter a plea to the charges and post bail. A preliminary hearing will follow and a judge will set a trial date. In the meantime, I want you to get examined by a physician as Mr. Thompson suggested earlier. If his assumption that there will be no sign of any medical procedure to correct your physical condition is correct, it will be crucial in the preparation of your defense."

Finch turned his attention to John Thompson, "So John, what can you do for us in this time?"

"I need to know the exact location of Mr. Scott's abduction. If the sight of his encounter is consistent with the other cases, there'll be unexplained impressions in the ground in that area. I want to investigate and take some photographs to document those markings while the imprints are still fresh."

"Good, I think I'll go with you. I'd like to see the site for myself. Mr. Scott, I'll be in contact with you later today. I'll have learned when your arraignment has been scheduled for by then."

Matt and Amy continued to share their feelings about the meeting with Finch and Thompson with one another. They knew that Matt's upcoming trial would be a challenge, but they felt comfort in the fact that Thomas Finch and John Thompson were on their side. Their thoughts then turned to the welfare of their son.

"Matt, I don't want to leave, but I've got to pick Jason up from school."

"Yeah, you better go. With all that's happening I almost forgot about him. Hopefully he hasn't had to deal with too much harassment yet."

Amy kissed Matt goodbye and hurried off to get Jason out of school.

Chapter 15

AMY ARRIVED AT THE SCHOOL and pulled into the parking lot. She exited her car and headed straight to the principal's office to get Jason and explain why she was removing him from school. She swiftly moved down the long hallway and as she entered the principal's office, she was surprised to see Jason sitting with one of the teachers. Jason saw Amy, jumped up and ran to meet her. She bent down and hugged him as he ran into her arms. Tears were streaming down his cheeks.

Although she already knew the answer to her question, she asked, "Jason honey, what's wrong?"

"Mommy all the kids are making fun of daddy. They say he's a space man. They say he's not really my daddy!"

The teacher that had been sitting with Jason approached Amy and explained that the children in his class had been teasing Jason about what had been reported on the previous evening's news cast.

"Mrs. Scott, although they don't mean to be, kids can be cruel. We thought it would be best to remove Jason from the classroom to avoid any more teasing about your husband's situation. The school tried to contact you, but there was no answer at your home."

"I was with my husband," Amy said as she looked at Jason, then back at the teacher. "I just came to get Jason and try to explain what's going on before... well before he heard it from the other kids. I guess I didn't get here in time. I really didn't think the news would travel as fast as it did."

"Under the circumstances, it's probably best that you take him home. Mrs. Scott, I don't know exactly what your situation is, but we have counselors available to you if you and Jason need to talk to someone."

Amy thanked the teacher for her concern as she took Jason by the hand and left the principal's office. When they reached the hallway Amy kneeled down and pulled Jason close as she did her best to console him.

"It's alright honey. We're going home and daddy will be there soon. It'll be okay, you'll see."

"I want daddy," was all he said as he tightly held onto Amy.

"I know honey, I know," she said softly as she rose to her feet, took Jason by the hand, and lead him to the exit at the end of the hallway.

Chapter 16

THE FOLLOWING AFTERNOON FINCH ACCOMPANIED Matt to his arraignment. He was presented with the charges against him to which he pleaded not guilty. Because of the strange circumstances of the case, the judge ordered Matt to undergo a psychological evaluation prior to the trial. Matt assured the judge that he understood his responsibility and was released after posting bail, pending the date of the trial.

Matt and Finch exited the courtroom, and as they walked down the courthouse steps, Matt expressed his joy to Finch that he would be going home to Amy and Jason. Matt and Amy decided it would be best for Jason if they moved back to their house rather than staying with Amy's sister. Their hope was that Jason would be less confused about Matt's return if they were all together again in the familiar surroundings of home.

Finch knew that Matt was anxious to get home, but he told him that they needed to make a stop on the way. As they drove away from the court house, Finch briefed Matt on the trek that he and John Thompson had taken to the abduction site. He revealed to Matt that Thompson was able to take photographs of the imprints in the ground, and that they matched the markings found at the two other sites.

"Matt, those photographs are key to building a case for your defense. We must compile and document any abnormality that we can link to your disappearance. Thompson is going to meet us at the site. He wants to go over your account of the abduction again."

"I'll tell him all that I can remember Thomas, but I don't think that there'll be any more than I have already told you."

"That's okay. The more often that you tell the story will prepare you for the court ordered psychological evaluation. You want to come across as sure of yourself as possible when the doctor interviews you. Matt, Thompson told us about the other two abduction cases that he's investigating. Do you remember having contact with any other humans during your abduction?"

"I remember images of other bodies lying still, seemingly floating on air, but I couldn't even tell you if they were male or female. I'm not even sure if they were human."

"That's exactly what the two others told Thompson when he first interviewed them. One of Thompson's associates is going to meet us at the site. His name is Robert Morrison. He's a clinical hypnotherapist who works with Thompson when he investigates abduction cases. Through hypnotherapy regression, the two other abductees were not only able to accurately describe one another; they also gave an accurate description of you."

Matt's eyes opened wide as he responded, "Me, really!"

"Yeah, evidently, while under hypnosis, they were able to clearly recall seeing one another, and you. That's pretty amazing, considering they live thousands of miles away from one another and had never met before. When we get there, he's going to try to put you under hypnosis. If all goes well, you'll be able to accurately describe the two other abductees, even though you've never seen them before, or should I say, even though you don't remember seeing them before."

Finch pulled the car to the side of the road when they reached the site of Matt's abduction. John Thompson and Robert Morrison were already there. Finch and Matt walked over to greet Thompson and were introduced to Morrison. Morrison explained that, through hypnosis, he hoped to bring to the surface any events of the abduction that Matt was unable to recall. He then proceeded to put Matt under hypnosis.

Morrison directed Matt to walk to the spot where his car had stalled on the day of his abduction and give a description of the event. Matt walked about 40 feet from the three men and stopped abruptly. Morrison approached him and asked questions that Matt answered from his Hypnotic state.

"I'm sitting here. The car is stalled." Matt points to a tree in front of him."That tree is beginning to shake." Without turning around, he refers to a dented guard rail behind him. "I look out the wind shield and see that my car has come to a stop against the guard rail on the side of the road. It's getting dark. The howling wind is shaking the car violently back and forth. The car is starting to rise from the ground. Everything is calm now. I seem to be getting pulled into an opening in some huge object above me. It's getting very bright as I get closer to the opening, much brighter I can't see anymore. The light is blinding," he said as he raised his hands, apparently in an attempt to shield his eyes from the light.

Matt's voice went silent as he lowered his arms and stood motionless. Finch started to walk toward him. Morrison raised his hand, signaling for Finch to halt.

"What happened? Why did he stop talking?" Finch asked.

"This is probably where he lost consciousness during the abduction," Morrison said.

Morrison went on to explain that in the other two cases, the abductees seemed to freeze up at this point in their hypnotic state. Within a few seconds they continued recounting details of their encounters as they responded to Morrison's questions. The accounts and descriptions given by both were eerily identical. Thompson told Finch that as Matt continued, if he was true to form, it would be as if Thompson was hearing the same account for the third time.

"The way things have gone to this point, I expect that I know exactly what Mr. Scott is going to say." Thompson said confidently.

"I hope so," Finch said. "Any information that we can get to support Matt's story will be of great help when he goes to trial."

Morrison continued to probe Matt's subconscious. "The light has dimmed now. What do you see?"

"I'm in a wide open area. I can't see any walls. There doesn't seem to be a floor or ceiling. It's very hazy. I see beams of soft amber colored light poking through the murky air. I feel a soothing effect as the light touches my skin, then envelops my entire body. The light is gone now, leaving me with a much energized sensation throughout my body. There are a lot of people moving around. I focus on their faces and they appear very odd looking. They have two eyes, but no nose, mouth or ears. They are hairless and have a very light grayish skin tone. They keep passing by, stopping occasionally, as if to examine me. I'm lying on my back with no visible support, as if I'm floating on air. I try to move, but all I can manage to do is turn my head from side to side. I can see two others that look like me.

"Can you describe the two others?" Morrison asked.

"They are also floating on air. There is a man and a woman. The woman is heavyset, fair skinned with short light brown hair. The man has a dark complexion. He has dark hair and a full beard. He is short and thin. He appears to be Middle Eastern. In the distance I can see what appear to be many more bodies floating in mid air, but they're too far away and all I can see are images. Two of the strange looking beings are coming toward me now. They're stopping and looking down at me. One of them is holding some type of device that he passes over my body once and then back again. I see and feel a very soothing amber beam of light. It's a much more intense light than I felt earlier and now everything is getting blurry. I'm starting to get very tired. It's getting dark."

Matt stood motionless and fell silent.

"Matt where are you now?" Morrison asked.

Matt gave no response to Morrison's question and remained statuesque.

"This is as far as we're going to get. It happened exactly this way with the two others. I've got to tell you," Morrison said to Finch and Thompson, "It sends a chill up my spine. We could have played a recording of the other two abductees and you would have heard the same account, almost word for word. It's uncanny!"

Morrison woke Matt from his trance and explained to him that under hypnosis he had given nearly the same details of his encounter as he had given to Thompson and Finch at their first meeting. He told Matt that his account however, was more detailed and included the descriptions of the aliens, as well as the two other abductees. He asked Matt if he could recall seeing the two other people now that he was not under hypnosis. Matt told Morrison that glimpses of two people flashed before his eyes, but he couldn't make out any distinct features. Thompson informed Matt and Finch that this was consistent with the others, and that probably, eventually Matt's subconscious would permit him to visualize his fellow abductees while in a conscious state.

Thompson and Finch decided to call it a day as they agreed that there was nothing more to be resolved at the abduction site. Before they departed, Finch questioned Thompson on the status of Matt's fellow abductees.

"John I'd like to interview the other abductees. Will you forward their contact information to me?"

"I will, but I think I can do better than that. They're here in the country. They agreed to come to my research Center after I contacted them about their encounters. I'm sure that I can set up a meeting with them. I was going to suggest bringing them and Matt together anyway. It seemed to be comforting for them to meet one another, and I'm sure it would have the same effect on Matt if he met them."

"John, you must be reading my mind," Finch said.

Finch thanked Thompson and made arrangements to contact him the following day. The men said their farewells as they departed the area.

Finch proceeded to drive Matt home. On the way he questioned Matt about the day of his return. He was curious in particular about the briefcase and its contents that were missing from Matt's car.

"Matt, when you first drove up to your house after the abduction, you knew that you were in possession of the funds belonging to the Willis/Cooper firm. Why didn't you take your brief case with you, or at least lock the door when you left the car?"

"I don't know Thomas. I just forgot about it. I was in such a hurry to see my wife that I couldn't think of anything else. I got out of the car, slammed the door shut and ran to the house."

Finch thought back to the police report. It had stated that when the police arrived at Matt's house to recover the car, the driver's side door was wide open.

"Are you positive that you closed the car door?"

"Yeah; why?"

"According to the police report, it was wide open when they arrived. That's interesting."

"How so?"

"Someone had to open the door after the police took you into custody. You said that you're sure that you closed it. I'll do some investigating into the police reports tomorrow. If they find fingerprints other than yours, it will prove that someone else was in the car."

Matt slumped back in his seat as he took a deep breath. Finch could see that he was overwhelmed by his situation and tried to console him.

"Matt I know that it's a lot to take in right now and I can see that you're worried, but try to look on the bright side. We're coming up with some pretty thought provoking, if not compelling arguments on your behalf. I feel much better about this case now than I did when I originally considered taking it on."

"Thanks Thomas. That makes me feel a little better…I guess."

Finch arrived at Matt's house and pulled into his driveway. He made arrangements to talk with Matt the following day and told Matt that there was something else that he would need from him.

"I need you to write down as exact as you remember the route that you took from work to home on the day of your abduction."

"Sure Thomas. Why?"

"If we can compare your company trip mileage report to the odometer in the car, and the distance traveled matches, it will show that the car wasn't driven anywhere other than that route. If that's the case, then the car would have been spotted and recovered by the police. After all, when you went missing they went over that route looking for the car. It'll be just one more piece of evidence to support your story when we get to court."

"I'll have it for you tomorrow Thomas," Matt said as he exited the car and waved as Finch gave him the thumbs up before driving away.

Chapter 17

As Matt walked toward the house, he saw Amy peering out of the front window anxiously awaiting his arrival. While walking up the front steps, the realization that he had not seen Jason in a year hit him like a ton of bricks. He wanted so badly to see his son, but he didn't know yet how to explain his absence. To tell Jason that he was abducted by aliens might scare the hell out of him, and if he made up some other excuse, how long could he shield him from the truth. He only had minutes to decide as Amy met him at the door. Matt walked into the house and pulled Amy into his arms. They held one another tight without speaking or a few moments before Amy broke the silence.

"It's good to have you home Matt."

"It's good to be home," Matt responded.

Matt kissed her then glanced around the nearly empty house. It looked so strange, devoid of the furniture and family pictures that used to inhabit the room.

"I almost forgot that I've been gone for a year. To me it still feels like only days."

"That must be really strange for you, but you're home now and hopefully we can get back to our normal lives."

"Speaking of normal lives, where's Jason? I'm dying to see him."

"He's in the backyard. I didn't call him when you pulled into the driveway because I thought that it might be best if you talked to me before you saw him. He took a lot of teasing from the kids at school and it really upset him. I should have kept him out of school until we could both sit down with him and try to explain the situation."

Matt nodded in agreement. Together they walked out the door leading to the backyard. Amy opened the door and called to Jason. Jason saw Matt, and after his young mind computed that his father was actually standing there, he started running toward him. Matt exited the house and scooped Jason up as he ran into his waiting embrace. A wide range of emotions overcame him as he held Jason tight. As great as the joy of holding his son was, it was diluted by the sorrow of knowing that he had missed a whole year of his young life. He told himself that he was home now. He was back with his wife and son, and for the moment, the world seemed right again. His elation was short-lived though as Jason spoke.

"Daddy the kids at school said that you ran away with the spacemen. Where did you go?"

Matt released Jason as he kneeled down and looked at him eye to eye.

"First of all, I want you to know that I would never run away from you, okay buddy?"

Jason nodded in response to Matt and listened intently as Matt continued.

"I had to go away with some special people to get well. These people fixed me up and made me feel better so I could run and play with you. It took them a long time to make me well again." Holding Jason at arm's length Matt continued. "Remember when you wanted to play ball in the backyard and I was hurt too much to play with you?"

"Yeah," Jason said. A wide eyed expression came over his face as he listened closely to Matt's every word.

"Now I'm all better. I can run and jump. We can play ball or tag you're it, or whatever you want. Doesn't that sound like fun?"

"Uh huh, are you gonna stay with me and mommy now? Don't go away again, okay daddy."

"I won't buddy, I won't," Matt said as he wrapped his arms around him and held him close to his chest.

Matt and Jason played in the back yard for the next hour. They took turns chasing one another in circles, occasionally tumbling to the ground and wrestling in the grass. Amy sat on the back steps, contently watching the playful interaction between father and son as the late afternoon turned to dusk. Matt stood with his hands resting on his knees. He patted Jason on the head as he struggled to catch his breath.

"Hey buddy, I just realized how big and strong you got. You're wearing me out."

Jason giggled as he ran at his dad in a playful attempt to push him to the ground. Matt caught him, and then fell back intentionally. He rolled over, jumped to his feet, and ran toward Amy. Jason scurried close behind. As they reached the stairs, Matt reached for Amy's hand and picked Jason up in his other arm and they entered the house as the squeaky screen door closed behind them.

Amy had sold most of their furniture when she decided to sell the house. Luckily there were still a couple of beds, a television and the table and folding chairs in the kitchen that hadn't been sold yet.

Amy rummaged through the kitchen cabinets looking for something to put together for dinner while Matt and Jason wrestled playfully, as they tumbled around on the living room floor. It was the most exercise Matt had gotten in a long time. He wiped drops of perspiration from his brow as he rolled over on his back.

"Hey buddy, what do you say we take a break while I catch my breath? I'll put the television on for you while I go see if mommy needs some help."

Matt lifted Jason from the floor and sat him in front of the TV, then returned to the kitchen, and as he put his arms around Amy, he glanced back at Jason.

"God, he's grown so much. I still feel like it's only been days since I've seen him. It's so depressing to realize that I've missed a whole year of his life."

Amy kissed Matt on the cheek and brushed her hand through his hair as she assured him that he would be able to make up for lost time now that they were a family again. She gently removed herself from Matt's embrace and continued to search the kitchen for something to eat. Amy opened the refrigerator door, and after surveying the contents, she looked back at Matt.

"I think we're out of luck, nothing in here except for a quart of milk, and it's almost empty. How about we order a pizza?"

"Sounds good to me; I haven't had a pizza in over a year. Come to think of it, I haven't had much of anything in over a year," he said in a half hearted joking manner.

Amy looked back at him with a wry smile as she placed the call to have a pizza delivered. Matt sat at the table staring out at Jason as he began to think about his upcoming trial and the expenses that would be incurred because of it. Amy hung up the phone and sat beside him.

"You're so quiet all of a sudden Matt. What are you thinking about?"

"Amy we're probably going to have to keep the house for sale. I don't have a job, and I'm sure our savings are really depleted. Who knows what expenses we're going to have now...with the legal costs and all."

"We'll be okay for a while, but you're right. I don't know how long we'll be able to keep paying the bills before the money runs out. Taking care of Jason and only working part time has made it really hard to keep up with the mortgage payments alone. Whatever happens, my sister offered to let us keep staying with her if we need to, at least until we get back on our feet."

"That's good to know."

Matt pulled his chair closer to Amy and lowered his voice so Jason wouldn't hear him.

"We've got to face the fact that I may be going to prison if a jury finds me guilty. I think we've got to start thinking about what you and Jason are going to do if that happens. How am I going to explain that to him? I already promised I wouldn't leave him again."

"Matt, let's not think about that right now. We just got you back in our lives and I can't bear to think about losing you again, not right now anyway."

"Okay, I guess I shouldn't let it eat away at me," Matt said as he put his hands on Amy's shoulders and pulled her close.

"Who knows, maybe at my psychological exam they'll think I'm nuts and put me in the loony bin instead of prison. At least you'll be able to come see me whenever you want."

Their conversation was interrupted by the doorbell. The pizza had arrived. Matt answered the door, paid for the pizza and brought it into the kitchen with Jason following close behind. Matt, Amy and Jason sat at the kitchen table and had their first meal together as a family in over a year. Matt and Amy talked and laughed with Jason and for the time being they set their problems aside and acted like a normal family. After dinner Jason ran off to watch TV while Matt helped Amy clear the table. Matt smiled as he watched his son disappear into the living room. "A regular Norman Rockwell moment huh," he said to Amy.

Amy grazed Matt's cheek with the palm of her hand. "I believe there's many more to come honey. I can just feel it."

They finished wiping off the dishes, then joined Jason in the living room, and spent the rest of the evening watching TV and enjoying their first night back together as a family.

The following morning Matt and Amy awoke as the sun pierced through the sheers that covered their bedroom window. Matt squinted as the sun's bright rays hit his eyes, and for a split second, he flashed back to the blinding light that he saw as he was pulled aboard the alien craft one year ago. The shock from the momentary flashback passed as he turned to see Amy lying next to him. He let out a sigh of relief, then kissed her and rose from the bed. Amy kicked the covers from her body and sat on the edge of the bed as she wiped the sleep from her eyes.

"What time do you have to see the psychiatrist today?"

"I've got to be at his office at 11 o'clock. Finch wants me to stop at his office first. I think he wants to make sure that I'm prepared for the evaluation process. I have to admit; having this doctor poke around in my head is a little nerve-racking."

"I'm sure it is, but think positive, maybe something good will come out of it."

"I hope so. Its court ordered, so I have no choice anyway. I have to do it whether I want to or not. I guess I'll take a shower and get myself ready."

Matt walked out of the bedroom and on his way to the bathroom, he stopped by Jason's room and peeked in at his son. Seeing that Jason was still asleep, he continued on. All he could think about was that this was the way he wanted every morning to start. He felt that if he kept that in mind, it would give him the strength that he needed to keep a positive attitude.

Matt walked out of the bathroom and toweled off his wet hair as he entered the kitchen. Amy and Jason had risen by now, and were sitting at the kitchen table. Amy poured a cup of coffee for Matt and herself. Matt took a sip as he gave Jason a pat on the head.

"I'm afraid there's not much for breakfast except maybe some left over cold pizza," Amy said.

"I used to live on that for breakfast when I was in college. What do you think Jason? MMM good," Matt said as he flipped open the pizza box and grabbed a slice before sliding it in front of Jason.

"Tomorrow something a little more nutritious," Amy responded as she looked down at Jason, then disapprovingly back in Matt's direction.

"My sister's coming over later to take Jason and I grocery shopping. I'll make us a good meal tonight."

"Sounds good, I guess I better get going. Don't want to keep the shrink waiting."

Matt gulped down the rest of his coffee, kissed Amy and gave Jason a pat on the head as he left to meet with Thomas Finch before going on to his psychological exam.

Chapter 18

MATT ARRIVED AT THE LAW office of Anderson and Finch. The receptionist informed him that Finch was waiting as she knocked on Finch's office door, opened it and directed Mat inside. Finch waved Matt in, then motioned for him to sit as he finished jotting down some notes on a pad of paper.

"How are you Matt?"

"Good as can be Thomas... under the circumstances."

"Just relax. That's the key to everything right now. The more at ease you seem to be, the more convincing your statements will come across during the evaluation. That's the main reason I wanted to see before you went there this morning. I think you'll be just fine."

"I hope you're right Thomas," Matt said, trying to sound confident.

"There is another thing that I wanted to talk to you about. John Thompson has set up a meeting with the two other abductees. You'll get to see them face to face."

"I've gotta tell you Thomas, as much as I look forward to that, it feels so strange that I'll actually be able to meet them. Until now I've only been able to see fleeting glimpses of them in my mind. It's been so aggravating because I see a mental picture of someone, but it's gone in a split second, and I can't seem to put a face with the image. I tell you though; it is going to feel good to talk to someone who knows what I've been through."

"I'm sure it will. I think this meeting will be very beneficial to you in many ways. My hope is that it will help you to attain a strong attitude and make you seem more confident of yourself when we're in the courtroom. I can't impress upon you enough, that how you come across to a jury is of the utmost importance."

"I understand Thomas. So when is our meeting with Thompson and the others?"

"I'm going to contact him later this morning to make the arrangements. In the meantime, I want to make sure that you get the psychological evaluation completed this morning. After you're done there, you need to make an appointment with your physician. We need to have him examine you and get current x-rays of your spine. We also need for him to examine your hair to confirm that it actually turned dark, and prove that you didn't color over the gray and we need to prove that your hair grew back in the areas that were balding. I'll need affidavits to support the results of his examinations when I begin to prepare your defense. That's all I've got for you this morning Matt; any questions?"

"No, I think I'm all set Thomas, thanks."

Finch wished Matt good luck and shook his hand as they rose from their chairs. Matt left Finch's office and made his way to the psychological exam. He was feeling more at ease with his situation in the knowledge that, even though he knew his story was so incredibly hard to accept, he had people fighting for and believing in him. His meeting with Finch left him confident that he would do well at the psychological examination.

Chapter 19

Amy and Jason were waiting for Matt to pick them up at Kathy's house. They had spent the day with her, shopping for food and other essentials that they would need now that they were back in their own home.

Matt pulled into Kathy's driveway. Jason saw him from the yard and ran to greet his dad. Matt kneeled down on one knee and caught him in his arms. Matt then released Jason and made a challenge to him.

"Come on little man. I'll race you to the house."

Jason giggled, turned and ran as fast as he could to the front steps with Matt jogging close behind. Amy and Kathy stood watching in amazement as Matt approached.

Amy turned to her sister. "Can you believe that Kathy? Matt could hardly walk a year ago, now he's running around like a deer."

"It is hard to believe, "Kathy said as she watched Matt moving toward them.

Matt put his arm around Jason's shoulder as they walked up the stairs leading to the front door. He kissed Amy as they entered the house. Kathy poured coffee for Matt, Amy and herself, and as they sat at the kitchen table, Amy anxiously waited for Matt to reveal the results of his evaluation.

"So how did it go today?" she asked impatiently.

"I think it went pretty well. At least the shrink didn't have me put in a straight jacket. I think that's a good sign," he said jokingly.

"Were you nervous?" Amy asked.

"Surprisingly no; I just answered his questions. We talked very little about the abduction. Almost all of the questions he asked were about how I felt before the abduction, our marriage, and life in general. I think he was just trying to determine if I'm stable enough to stand trial. All in all, it seemed to go pretty well. I'll know more after Finch gets the results."

Matt and Amy finished their coffee, and as the conversation dwindled, they gathered their groceries, said goodbye to Kathy and left for home.

Matt turned off the main road on to the street where they lived. Jason sat in the back seat, holding Amy's undivided attention, as she sat facing him, while helping him along with the school work that he would miss out on by not being in class. Their house came into view as Matt passed by the cars that lined both sides of the street. Something captured his attention as he drove closer to the house. He noticed a large object propped against the lamppost on the front lawn. He pulled into the driveway and at close range he could see that it was a figure of what someone had imagined an alien being would look like. It was cut out of card board and placed on the lawn. In the hand of the figure was a sign reading, "take me to your leader". Matt let out a disgruntled sigh as he tapped Amy's shoulder to get her attention, then pointed to the cardboard cutout.

"I wondered when this would start happening. Thompson warned me that Jason wouldn't be the only one held up to ridicule. He told me to be prepared for this kind of prank."

Amy responded with a concerned look on her face and a nervous tone in her voice.

"Let's hope this is as far as it goes. I'm worried about how the other kids are going to treat Jason when he goes back to school."

Amy diverted Jason's attention from the cardboard figure as she rushed him past it and into the house. Matt tore it away from the lamppost and held it in front of him at arm's length. He looked it over for a few seconds, and as he ripped into pieces that would fit into the trash can, he thought to himself, "they didn't even look anything like this". He stuffed the torn up cardboard into the garbage can and looked up toward the sky as he approached the back door. He expressed his next thought out loud as he opened the door, his eyes still fixed on the heavens. "It sure would make things easier if you guys would return." Matt halfheartedly waited for a response, and then entered the house, pulling the screen door shut behind him. He entered the kitchen where Amy was preparing dinner while Jason sat in the living room watching television. They were settling back into the normal routine that they were accustomed to before the abduction. Amy put dinner on the table as she summoned Jason to the kitchen, and the family sat down to eat. After dinner, Amy cleared the kitchen table while Matt and Jason roughhouse on the living room floor as they watched one of Jason's favorite television shows. It was probably the most normal evening they had spent together as a family since Matt's return.

Later that evening, after putting Jason to bed, Matt and Amy relaxed on the front porch swing. It was a dark night, void of clouds, with thousands of bright stars scattered across the sky. Amy rested her head on Matt's shoulder as she gazed into the night. Out of the dark abyss, a shooting star streaked across the sky. She was startled by the sudden appearance of the bright ball of light, and as it caught her attention she pointed toward the sky.

"Matt, did you see that?"

"Yeah," Matt answered, as he watched the star's fading path disappear into the night. "Strange how rarely we see one of those." He paused, "From now on, anytime I see something moving around out there, I'm gonna wonder if it's just a meteoric rock, or my friends making a return trip. It's kinda creepy every time I see a flickering light in the sky."

Amy looked up at Matt and responded with a curious tone in her voice.

"I wonder if they're around us all the time, observing us. Do they randomly abduct people, or do they have an agenda?"

"Who knows," Matt answered as he gazed out at the stars.

"You and the two others all had serious physical problems. Do you think they took you away knowing that they were going return you in perfect health?"

Matt shrugged his shoulders as he responded to Amy.

"It's strange. I've been wondering about that ever since I returned. Do they really take us knowing that they're going to cure us, or are we just lab rats to them? Maybe they're using experimental procedures on us before they use them on their own kind. I wonder if I got a bonus though," he said as he brushed his hand through his now thick, dark brown hair.

"What do you mean?" Amy asked.

"I was going gray and balding. Now look at me."

Amy laughed as she ran her fingers through his hair. "I do like that. We'll have to thank them if they ever return."

They sat back in the swing for a little while longer, swaying back and forth as they stared up at the heavens. Growing weary, they decided to retire for the evening. It was getting late, and Matt wanted to be well rested for the next day. He would be meeting with the doctor to discuss the results of his X-rays, then on to meet with Finch to plan strategy for his upcoming trial.

Chapter 20

MATT'S RESTLESS MIND WOKE HIM early the next morning. He glanced at the clock on the night stand and saw that there was still time before the alarm would sound. He lay still, staring at the ceiling as thoughts of how Finch would defend him in court raced through his mind. He thought about how he would react if he was one of the jurors listening to a lawyer defend a client who claimed to have been abducted by aliens. He thought that it would have to be one good attorney, and hopefully Finch was that lawyer.

The alarm finally sounded, and as Amy wiped the sleep from her eyes, she turned to Matt.

"Good morning honey, how'd you sleep?" she asked as she cuddled up next to him.

"Okay I guess. I woke up a few times during the night. Each time it felt like this whole alien encounter experience was just a dream."

"I can't imagine what you must be going through," Amy said as she slid her hand up Matt's arm and brushed her fingers across his cheek.

"You know it's kind of funny in a strange way. I used to hear about people making claims of UFO sightings, and I thought they were probably just seeing weather balloons or our own aircraft. Either that or they were just nuts. Now I'm one of those people, and I'm sure other people think I'm out of my mind."

Amy kissed Matt on the cheek and gave him a reassuring hug. "I don't think you're crazy. John Thompson believes in you to. So does Thomas Finch or he wouldn't have taken your case."

"Well that's nice to hear, but the people on the jury are going to have to agree or nothing else matters."

Matt paused and looked into Amy's eyes, then continued with an apologetic tone in his voice.

"I didn't mean that the way it sounded. What matters most to me is what you believe, no matter what happens in court."

"I know," Amy said as she kissed Matt, and then slipped out from under the covers.

"I'll put some coffee on and start breakfast."

Matt swept the covers away from his body and rose to a standing position. He noticed his image in the mirror and was amazed at how erect he stood. He was so used to seeing the image of a hunched over body because of the constant pain that traveled from his back, through his hips, and into his knees. A sheepish grin came over his face as he exited the bedroom and thought to himself, "At least I've got my health."

The aroma of bacon, eggs and coffee wafted through the air, drawing Matt into the kitchen. Amy was preparing Jason for school as they sat at the kitchen table. It would be his first day back since the other kids had mercilessly teased him about his father's predicament. Matt sat next to Jason and fumbled for words of encouragement to prepare him for the harassment that he might have to endure throughout the day.

"Hey pal, are you ready to go back to school today?"

Jason responded with a shrug of his shoulders as he chewed on a piece of toast. Matt put his hand on Jason's arm and squeezed it gently as he continued.

"The kids at school were pretty tough on you huh."

Jason looked up at Matt as he shrugged his shoulders again. Matt kneeled down on the floor in front of him and looked at him eye to eye.

"Is there anything that you want to talk to me about, anything you want to ask me?"

Matt waited for a response. Jason looked to the floor as he pondered Matt's question. He had a look of bewilderment on his face as he looked back into Matt's eyes.

"Daddy, the kids said it's all make-believe. They said you lied about the spacemen. Nicky Martin said his daddy told him that you ran away cause you didn't love us anymore. All the kids were laughing at you. They say you're just a big liar."

Matt pulled Jason toward him and hugged him tightly. Amy pulled a chair close to them and sat as she wiped a tear from her cheek. Matt gently moved Jason out to arms length.

"Buddy, I would never lie to you. Everything that I told you is true. You just have to believe me. I know it's going to be hard at school, and some of the kids are going to say things that aren't very nice, but you've got to try and ignore them. Do you think you can do that?"

Jason nodded yes, but his body language was far from convincing. Matt knew that the more publicity that his situation attracted, the more humiliating it could get for Jason. He gave Jason a kiss on the forehead, then sat back down in his chair as Amy put their breakfast on the table.

They began to eat when their breakfast was interrupted by the doorbell. Matt motioned for Amy to stay seated and went to answer the door. As he opened the door, and a man holding a camera moved to the top of the stairs and snapped his picture. Another man shoved a microphone in his face.

"Mr. Scott, Ron Jarret, from the National Recorder. Can you tell me about the abduction? What did the aliens look like?"

Matt was caught off guard. Even though John Thompson had warned him that the tabloids would be looking to exploit his story, he didn't expect them to come knocking at his door. The reporter continued to fire questions at him. Bearing in mind that Thompson had warned him that anything he would say to these people could be misconstrued, or even worse, intentionally twisted to present their story in the most sensationalistic way, he stopped short of answering any questions. "No comment, please leave." He stepped back and closed the door as the reporter persistently tried to get a response to his questions while the photographer kept snapping pictures. Matt moved toward the window and peered through the drapes as he watched the reporters walk back to their car. Sure that they were gone, he walked back to the kitchen.

"Who was at the door?" Amy asked.

Matt responded nonchalantly, careful not to use a tone that might upset Jason.

"You're not going to believe it… You know that rag that masquerades as journalism, the National Recorder?"

"You're kidding," Amy said excitedly.

Matt leaned toward Jason, "hey buddy how about you go get your books. The school bus will be here soon."

"Okay dad," Jason said as he took a sip of his orange juice, and then ran off to get his books.

"Thompson told me to expect this, but I really didn't think they'd come to the house."

"What can we do about it?"

"Nothing; unless they do something that's against the law, they can harass us as much as they want to."

The sound of a vehicle coming to a stop in front of the house caught their attention. Matt cautiously opened the door and looked out to the street. Seeing only the school bus, he quickly surveyed the area to make sure that the reporters were gone. Amy came out with Jason and waved goodbye as he entered the school bus. They walked back into the house and sat down to have one more cup of coffee before Matt left for his appointment with his physician, then on to meet with Thomas Finch and John Thompson.

Chapter 21

MATT ARRIVED AT DR. RAYFORD's office earlier than his scheduled appointment. As he sat in the waiting room, eagerly awaiting the results of his x-rays, he wondered how the vertebrae that were in such a bad state of deterioration before his abduction would look now. A few minutes passed before the receptionist called him in to see the doctor. Matt was seated as the doctor walked into the examining room.

"Hi Doc, how ya doing?" Matt asked.

"I'm doing fine, but you…"

Dr. Rayford looked into Matt's eyes as he raised his hands in the air. His expression was one of total amazement.

"Never in my twenty five years of practicing medicine have I ever seen anything like this. The last time I saw you, you were the most likely candidate for back surgery that I had ever seen. Your spine was in such a state of degeneration, that without surgery, you would have eventually been confined to a wheelchair. I'm sure of it."

Dr. Rayford paused as he removed Matt's x-rays from a large manila envelope and pressed them against a lighted screen to show the skeletal makeup of Matt's spine.

"Your X-rays show that your spine is in perfect alignment. The vertebrae are in perfect position, and there is no wear on the discs. There's no indication that you ever went through a procedure to correct any abnormal condition that may have existed. I don't understand how that's possible. Some type of procedure must have been performed on your back, and yet I see no scar tissue. It just doesn't make any sense. I had to call the lab to confirm that these really were your x-rays."

Dr. Rayford paused, and then addressed Matt curiously. "Matt I need you to take off your shirt so I can examine your back."

Matt removed his shirt and Dr. Rayford looked closely for any indication that an operation was performed. He was amazed to find that, not only was there no scar tissue on the x-rays of Matt spine, there was also no sign of incisions on his body that would have been made during an operation. He sat down and shook his head in awe as he looked Matt in the eye.

"This is the most astonishing thing I've ever seen."

"Doc, I'm just as amazed as you are. I'm pain free and I can move around like I did when I was a teenager. There's another strange thing that happened to me. My grey hair has turned dark and the bald spot on top of my head is covered with hair again, just like it was twenty years ago. My lawyer is going to need proof that it actually turned dark and I didn't dye it this color."

Dr. Rayford plucked a hair from Matt's scalp and studied it under a magnifying glass, then looked back at Matt.

"The last time I saw you, your hair was prematurely gray. If you had died your hair, the roots would still be gray, but they're dark brown. We age and our hair turns gray. What it doesn't do is turn back to its natural color again. That's not how our body chemistry works. I have no logical explanation for what's happened to you."

Dr. Rayford jotted some notes down on Matt's chart and as they conversed, something in Matt's history caught his eye. He looked quizzically back at Matt.

"That red mark on your neck," he said as he lifted Matt's chin and examined his neck. "My chart shows that I removed a mole from that spot over a year ago. I even remember doing the procedure. I don't know why that area hasn't healed yet. It should have scared over and completely cleared up within a couple of weeks. If I didn't know better I'd say that the procedure was done only days ago. That's very strange."

"Doc, I've experienced a lot of strange things lately."

"I've got to admit, when I first heard about your claim to have been abducted by aliens, I was more concerned about your mental health than I was about your physical problems. Now I don't know what to think. I can't explain the miraculous changes that I've seen in you. I guess we have to consider all possibilities, alien intervention included."

"I'm glad to hear you say that. I'm going to need as many open-minded people on my side as possible when my case goes to trial. You do realize that you're going to be subpoenaed to appear in court."

"Matt, after reading about you in the newspaper, then seeing these x-rays, I knew that most likely I would be called on to provide the results of my examination. I'd be more than happy to testify on your behalf. I don't know what to think about alien encounters, but I do know that medical science as we know it has no explanation for the transformation that has taken place in your body. I hope the results of my examination will be useful in your defense."

"Thanks Doc. That's comforting to hear."

Dr. Rayford finished his examination and shook Matt's hand as they walked out to the reception area together. Matt thanked him and left the office for his meeting with Thomas Finch and John Thompson. He was becoming increasingly excited about the meeting with the two other people that had been abducted.

Matt arrived at the law office. The receptionist let Finch know that he had arrived and directed him to Finch's office. Finch opened door and welcomed Matt in.

"Hi Matt; come in. We're all here," Finch said as he put his hand on Matt's shoulder and lead him into the room. He motioned for Matt to sit in an empty chair next to Thompson. On the other side of Thompson sat the two people who shared Matt's alien encounter. Finch walked around his desk and sat down. Thompson turned to Matt, rose to his feet, and shook his hand as he began to make the introductions. Matt's jaw dropped, and his knees weakened as he took a good look at his fellow former abductees. Thompson took hold of his arm and eased him into his chair as he commented, "You look like you've seen a ghost Matt."

Matt swallowed a lump that had formed in his throat caused by the excitement of the moment.

"Not a ghost, but close to it. I remember your faces so vividly now," he said as he stared at the two strangers.

The two people rose from their chairs and walked over to Matt. They were all overwhelmed by the moment and the three strangers hugged as if they were long-lost relatives. Thompson stood and addressed Matt.

"I'd like to introduce you to, or let me rephrase that. I'd like to re-introduce you to Alice Harrison, and Raj Patel. Alice, Raj, this is Matthew Scott. Raj and Alice have agreed to testify in your behalf. They're thrilled, as I know you are, to meet another person who has shared their experience. I have interviewed the three of you separately and I find it remarkable that your descriptions of the encounters are the same down to the smallest details. What makes that even more remarkable is the fact that you had never met, before or after the abductions, until we brought you together today. I think sworn testimony to that effect will bolster Matt's chances in court. What do you think Thomas?"

Finch folded his hands behind his head as he leaned back in his chair. A wide smile covered his face as he sat beaming with an air of confidence.

"I never thought in a million years that I would be taking on a case like this. Maybe I should say, I never thought that I would take on a case like this with such confidence. I'm really starting to like our chances."

Finch's statement was music to Matt's ears. He felt that Finch was on his side all along, but for the first time he was confident that Finch truly believed his story. For the rest of the afternoon Raj, Alice and Matt shared their thoughts of the time that they spent with the aliens and how it had affected their lives so far. Thompson and Finch sat and observed as the three of them discussed their encounters. Memories that were only brought to the surface under hypnosis began to trickle into their conscious minds to the point that they were finishing one another's thoughts as they expressed them out loud.

The meeting went as well or better than Finch could have hoped for. He had been concerned that at the trial, Raj Patel and Alice Harrison would be useless to Matt's defense if they came across as less than normal and emotionally stable. Other than claiming to have been abducted by aliens, their demeanor was that of ordinary well adjusted people.

The afternoon hours had slipped away, and as the evening hours approached, the group brought their meeting to a close. Matt, Alice and Raj were physically and mentally spent. The meeting left them with a wide range of emotions, from the thrill of meeting one another, to the feeling of loss for the year in time that they were separated from their families and loved ones. It was a year that would forever leave a void in their lives. The three of them hugged one another and vowed to stay in contact after the trial. In the short time that they had spent together, a bond had been formed that only they could fully understand. They were from different backgrounds, different parts of the world, and had very little in common except for the out of this world experience that they shared.

Thompson escorted Alice and Raj to the hotel where they would be staying as Finch and Matt settled back down in Finch's office.

"So what do you think Thomas?" Matt asked.

"After seeing the three of you together, and with all the evidence to support your case, I don't know how a jury could dismiss the idea that your story isn't at least plausible. That reminds me. I met with the judge and prosecuting attorney this morning. We made the jury selection and I'm very happy with our choices."

"That's good to hear Thomas. I just hope they'll be open-minded."

"That's all we can ask Matt. Now it's my job to sway them over to our side."

Finch placed his hand on Matt's shoulder as he walked him to the reception area. He could see that Matt was drained from the emotional meeting with his fellow abductees.

"Go home and get some rest Matt. The best thing that you can do for yourself now is to just kick back and relax. I know that sounds impossible, but do anything that you can to get your mind off the trial. We need you to be as sharp as possible when the prosecuting attorney questions you in court."

"I'll try Thomas," Matt said as he did his best to sound positive while shaking Finch's hand. He walked out of the office, turned and waved to Finch as he exited the building and headed for home.

Chapter 22

AMY HAD BEEN ANXIOUSLY WAITING for Matt's arrival. She heard a car pull into the driveway and walked out to the front step to greet him. They kissed and she reached for Matt's hand. "So tell me all about it," she said, referring to Matt's meeting at Finch's office.

"It was weird. I've never met these people and yet I recognized them instantly. They were as familiar to me as someone I had known all my life would be. Their names are Raj Patel and Alice Harrison. We felt a connection as soon as we met. It felt so good to talk with other people who had shared my experience. They know how it feels to have lost a whole year of your life."

Amy hugged Matt, and then took him by the hand as they entered the house and walked into the kitchen. Matt sat down. Amy poured two cups of coffee, and then joined him at the kitchen table. It was the first time all day that Matt had a chance to relax. He was mentally exhausted, but pleased that things had gone so well. He took a sip of coffee then glanced toward his son's room.

"Where's Jason? I thought maybe I'd play a little ball with him."

"He's at Kathy's house. I thought it might be best if he stayed there tonight. She volunteered to take care of him and I thought it would be less confusing for him. You know, with us talking about the trial and all. Besides, he likes being with her; you know how she spoils him."

"Yeah I guess that's probably a good idea. I'll have plenty of time to spend with him when it's all over. Listen to me, Mr. confident all of a sudden."

Amy looked across the table at Matt and smiled at him approvingly as she responded to his comment.

"It seems with every day that passes, there's more reason to be confident. I think things are going to work out just fine. I can feel it. Now why don't you go watch TV and relax. I'll make a couple of sandwiches and bring them into the living room.

"You're too good to me," Matt said as he rose from the table and walked into the other room. He turned the TV on, plopped down onto a chair and began watching the evening news. A few minutes later Amy entered the room carrying the sandwiches that she made only to find Matt passed out in his chair. She thought about waking him, but he looked so peaceful that she couldn't bring herself to disturb him. She brought the sandwiches back to the kitchen, then returned to the living room and covered Matt with a blanket. She then sat in the chair next to him and halfheartedly watched the evening news as she studied the expression on Matt's face. She wondered what kind of dreams haunted his subconscious as he lay there sleeping. Surely his mind must be dealing with the aftermath of his alien encounter.

The evening progressed and Matt's peaceful sleep was only interrupted by an occasional snore. Amy, not wanting to go to bed until Matt awoke, grabbed a blanket and curled up in the chair next to him. The flickering light emitting from the television seemed to have a hypnotic effect, and as her eye lids grew heavy, she also drifted off to sleep.

Matt and Amy awoke simultaneously as the morning sun lit up the living room. They both stretched to relieve the kinks from their bodies, caused by sleeping awkwardly in the living room chairs. Matt leaned over, kissed Amy, and then sprung into his feet. Amy sat back and smiled, still amazed at how effortlessly Matt moved as he rose from the chair.

"I'm still not used to seeing you get up that fast. You used to slowly roll out of bed before making it to your feet."

"Yeah, it sure is nice to be able to pop right up, no pain at all."

Amy rose from her chair and walked toward the kitchen.

"I'll put some coffee on."

She stopped in the doorway and looked back in Matt's direction. "So what's on the agenda for today?"

"Just waiting to hear from Finch. He's meeting with John Thompson this morning. After that he's going to meet with Willis/Cooper's lawyer for the pretrial hearing. Hopefully everything will go smoothly and the judge will set a trial date. Finch said he'd call sometime this afternoon, as soon as the pretrial hearing is over."

Amy continued into the kitchen with Matt close behind.

"Why is Finch meeting with John Thompson again so soon?"

"He told me that Thompson's organization was involved in some other investigations that might be pertinent to my case. How I don't know, but I welcome any help that I can get."

"I guess so," Amy responded, "coffee?"

Matt slid his cup toward Amy. She poured a cup for both of them and they went into the living room to watch the morning news on television. Good morning Chicago, a morning news and talk show, was just beginning. The hosts of the show did the normal talk show segments, news, weather, sports and conversation about current events. Matt's attention was divided between what came on the TV screen and thoughts of Finch's meeting with the judge and the prosecuting attorney at the pretrial hearing that morning. The hour-long show was coming to a close as one of the hosts presented her final story.

"Well," she said in a scathing tone. "We have a follow up to a snippet that was on the evening news last week. A man from the Creekview suburb of Chicago claimed to be abducted by aliens."

The woman's comment caught Matt's attention. He reached for the TV remote and turned up the volume as he and Amy exchanged glances, and then looked back at the TV screen.

The TV personality continued on, "It seems allegedly, that this guy disappeared a year ago with funds belonging to his employer. He's back now and his defense is."

She paused as a sarcastic smirk came over her face and she shook her head in disbelief.

"Get this. He says aliens held him aboard a UFO against his will. They brought him back but, hmmm, they must have taken the money that he vanished with because he doesn't know what happened to it. How about that, thieves from outer space. Can you believe that they are actually taking this case to trial?"

She looked toward her co-host as the screen widened to show both of them. He shuffled some paper in his hands as they both chuckled at the story.

"It takes all kinds, see you tomorrow folks," he said as the show came to a close.

A dumbfounded expression came over Matt's face as he leaned back in his chair, still clutching the TV remote. Amy leaned toward him and slipped her hand in his.

"They don't paint a very flattering picture of you do they?"

"No, they make me sound like some kind of nut, and a thief on top of that. Of course what can I expect? That's what I'd think to if I heard my story. I can only imagine what the jury members were thinking when they got picked for this trial."

"Have faith Matt. Finch told you that he was satisfied with the jurors that were selected."

Amy moved close and put her arms around Matt as she tried her best to console him. She could sense how detrimental the TV personality's comments were to his positive attitude. A range of emotions rushed through his mind. Thomas Finch and John Thompson had provided him with positive reinforcement, but now he was getting to see the other side of the coin. He could see the ridicule and doubt that would probably torment him throughout the whole ordeal. He had been up and down on a roller coaster ride of emotions, and this was one of those down times.

Amy kissed him on the cheek, and then eased back into her chair.

"Matt you've got to remember that those people on TV don't know the facts. They haven't heard the evidence in your favor. Of course they're going to react like they did."

"Yeah, I guess you're right. It's just that Finch and Thompson have been pumping me up so much that I almost forgot how ridiculous my story sounds."

"Matt, you're right. It does sound ridiculous, and that's what I thought when I first heard it from you that day at the county jail. I just wanted to get away from you. I was mad and hurt by what I thought was a crazy story, but then little by little, evidence came out to support your claims and I was convinced that you were telling the truth. I feel in my heart, that when Finch presents the evidence in court, the jury will have to consider that it could be true."

Matt stood up and took Amy by the hand. A sheepish smile came across his face as he pulled her close and whispered, "How'd you get so smart?"

Amy shrugged her shoulders in response to his question that really needed no verbal answer. The roller coaster ride of emotions was now climbing back, slowly but steadily, to the top of its apex.

It was well into the afternoon. Amy had gone to Kathy's house to get Jason. Matt paced back and forth from the kitchen to the living room; glancing at the telephone each time he walked by. He was anxious to hear from Finch about how the pretrial hearing went. Minutes seemed like hours as he peeked at his watch repeatedly. The telephone finally rang and Matt rushed to answer it with restless anticipation as he saw Finch's number on the caller ID.

"Hello Thomas."

"Hi Matt, how are you?"

"Okay I guess, anxious to hear how things went today."

"I thought you might be. Everything is a go. The judge set a trial date for two weeks from today. There have also been some new developments since yesterday. Some quite significant ones I might add."

Matt could sense the exuberance in Finch's voice as he listened intently.

"Matt your briefcase was recovered yesterday. The police took four men into custody. The four of them have been involved in car thefts and home invasions in your neighborhood. The fingerprints found in your car matched the prints of one of those men. Some of the money and all of the checks were still in their possession."

Matt was elated to hear the news. His heart was racing as he responded before Finch could continue.

"So what does that all this mean Thomas? It's good, right. I mean doesn't that prove that I didn't steal the money?"

"That the stolen money was recovered is good news. On one hand we know that the briefcase containing the missing funds was stolen from your car, and we have the evidence to prove that, as well as evidence to prove who took it. On the other hand, the prosecution is making the argument that for one whole year, you were in possession of those funds. They'll contend that whatever happened to those funds while in your possession, is after-the-fact, and therefore irrelevant. They'll make the case that the trial is about the felony charges against only you, and the fact that another crime was committed is a separate issue. That being said, if we can convince the jury that your abduction story is at least plausible, then they must consider the possibility that your intention was to make the bank deposit on your way home from the office as planned on the day of your encounter. The prosecution's argument that you kept the missing funds in your possession for a year will be a point of debate. We'll argue that the length of time of your disappearance, subsequent to your abduction was out of your control; therefore your intention was to make the bank deposit as planned. The more the judge allows us to work that into your defense, the better off we'll be. That brings me to the other thing that happened today."

"What's that Thomas?" Matt said, doing his best to absorb everything that Finch was telling him.

"I talked to John Thompson before the hearing this morning. Apparently Raj Patel, Alice Harrison and you may not have been the only people to have experienced an alien encounter. Thompson's agency has learned of other cases like yours. His investigators have been contacted by over 20 people whose claims of alien encounters mirror those of Raj, Alice and you. All have been gone for the same period of time and returned on the same date. All have also returned with a miraculous recovery from some type of physical ailment."

"Twenty people you say Thomas?"

"Twenty and counting. The publicity that your story has generated is coaxing people, who were afraid and embarrassed, to now come forth with their experiences. I presented this information at the pretrial this morning and, if as Thompson suspects, new stories will keep filtering in. I believe the judge will allow us to offer these new stories at the trial as evidence in your behalf."

Finch paused as he waited for a response, and then continued, "Matt do you have any questions about what I've told you so far?"

Matt responded with apprehension in his voice.

"I can't think of anything right now Thomas. I've got all this stuff bouncing around in my head but I'm sure I'll have some questions once everything sinks in."

"That's exactly what I would expect your reaction to be Matt. I know that I'm throwing a lot of information at you all at once. I recommend that you sit back and gather your thoughts. We'll talk again tomorrow."

"Thanks Thomas. Goodbye"

Matt put the phone down and collapsed in his chair. He wondered if the alien encounter story that Finch would be using as the cornerstone of his defense would be enough to convince the jury of his innocence, or if they would see it as some extravagant story to cover up a crime. He felt some relief in the fact that Finch had a clear cut direction in preparing for his defense and that he showed confidence in presenting his case to a jury. All he could do now was wait for his day in court.

Matt spoke with Finch every day over the next two weeks leading up to the trial. Finch wanted to keep him abreast of any developments in John Thompson's investigations concerning cases of new abductees, along with any changes in strategy for his defense. Most of all he wanted to keep Matt in a positive frame of mind. Matt would need to exude confidence and be as convincing as possible to increase his chances of an acquittal when presenting his story to the jury.

Matt has was surprisingly tranquil in the two weeks leading up to the trial. The anxiety that had consumed his emotions was gone. It might be because he knew that all the preparation had been done, and there was nothing left to do but present his case. It might be that he had come to terms with the fact that a guilty-not guilty verdict was out of his hands, and all he could do now was have faith that the jury would accept the fact that his story was at least a possibility.

It was the eve of the trial date. Matt lay in bed with Amy cuddled up beside him. His mind was clear as he stared at the blades of the ceiling fan slowly rotating above him. It had a mesmerizing effect that eased him into a restful sleep that would consume the night and leave him refreshed for the following day.

The next morning Amy awoke and turned to see that Matt had already risen from bed. She could hear the water running from the shower in the adjoining bathroom. She rose from bed and slipped into her bathrobe as Matt exited the bathroom while toweling off his wet hair.

"Morning dear," Amy said as she passed by Matt on her way out of the bedroom. Matt followed her into the kitchen and sat down as Amy started the coffee maker.

"Big day today dear, are you getting nervous?" she asked timidly.

"No. I don't understand why, but I feel pretty good, like it's going to be okay."

"That's great," Amy said, pleased to see that Matt was in a good frame of mind.

"Well I'm not in court yet. I hope I still feel this way when I walk through those courtroom doors."

Amy put her arms around Matt as she stood over him and kissed the top of his head. "You will dear. I can feel it."

Chapter 23

Later that morning Finch escorted Matt and Amy to the federal court. He felt confident that he had Matt well prepared as he went over last-minute instructions. They pulled into the parking lot, exited the car and started to walk toward the courthouse. Matt paused with his eyes fixed on the stairs leading up to the large gray building where his fate would be decided. A touch of nervousness came over him as he realized the finality of his ordeal. Finch observed the look of concern on Matt's face. He moved to his side and put his hand on Matt's shoulder as he spoke with a reassuring tone in his voice.

"It's okay Matt. We're well prepared for what awaits us in there."

"I believe you Thomas. I just wish my friends from out there were here to verify my story," he said as he pointed his finger up at the sky.

"Yeah, I'll admit, that wouldn't hurt our case any," Finch said. He smiled and nodded in agreement as they walked up the courthouse steps and entered the building.

Matt and Finch entered the courtroom and sat at a table facing the judge's chair and witness stand. Off to the side was the juror's box where the seven men and five women who would determine his fate had just been seated. He glanced over at an adjacent table and saw the prosecuting attorney and his ex-employer, Alan Cooper. It was the first time he had seen Cooper since the day he left the office over a year ago. His first impulse was to approach him and try to offer an explanation for his disappearance. After all, his relationship with this man had been more than employer/employee. They had been friends. The realization that the friendship was over was soon confirmed when Cooper looked toward him with a cold stare that turned into a scowl of disgust as he turned away from Matt. Cooper's reaction should have been no surprise to Matt, and yet to actually experience it was a sobering feeling. He turned his attention away from the prosecution and scanned the crowded courtroom for a friendly face. Amy caught his eye as she smiled and raised her hand, giving him a slight wave so he would know she was there. Her presence brought about a comforting feeling, and he responded with a quick nod of acknowledgement before turning his attention back toward the juror's box.

The doors to the judge's chambers opened and the court room went quiet. Everyone rose as the bailiff announced the judge's entrance.

"All rise. The Court of Cook County is now in session. The Honorable Judge Walter Nathan is presiding."

Everyone remained standing as the judge was seated. The judge instructed the room to be seated, and then addressed the bailiff.

"Mr. Sims, what is today's calendar?"

"Your Honor, today's case is the Willis/Cooper advertising agency versus Mr. Matthew Scott."

The judge then turned his attention first, to the prosecuting attorney, then to Finch and asked if each party was ready to begin trial. They both responded with, "Yes your honor". He next addressed the jury with his final instructions.

"Good morning ladies and gentlemen. Thank you for sacrificing your time today. Ladies and gentlemen of the jury, you must remember that you are to base your conclusions on the evidence as presented throughout this trial, and that the opening and closing arguments of the lawyers are not to be construed as evidence. If that is understood, we shall proceed."

The jury foreman assured the judge that his instructions were understood. Judge Nathan, being satisfied that all were ready to begin, instructed the attorneys to give their opening statements. The prosecution was first to act. The prosecuting attorney walked toward the jury, stopped and folded his hands, as he began to speak.

"May it please the court, and ladies and gentlemen of the jury. My name is Michael Robbins, counsel for the Willis/Cooper advertising agency in this action. Throughout this trial, you will hear the defense speak of the defendant's supposed alien encounter as the reason for his disappearance with funds belonging to the Willis/Cooper advertising agency. They will attempt to convince you of his alleged abduction. To tell you the truth, this court doesn't really care if you believe his story or not. It does not matter. You must remember that this case is not about whether or not you believe his incredible tale. It is about only the embezzlement of property and funds that were in Mr. Scott's possession on the day he disappeared over one year ago. Those funds are the property of the Willis/Cooper Advertising Agency, and were entrusted into Mr. Scott's care to deposit into the firm's financial institution on the day that he disappeared. It has been established, as you will see, that those funds were in Mr. Scott's possession for a full year after the day that said funds were to be deposited into the firm's corporate account. I intend to prove to you, the jury, that Matthew Scott is guilty of the charges of embezzlement and grand theft."

Robbins finished with his opening statement and returned to the prosecution's table. Finch rose and addressed the jury with his opening statement.

"Your honor, members of the jury, my name is Thomas Finch, counsel for Mr. Matthew Scott in this action. It is true that this case is not about the alien abduction that you will be hearing so much about throughout this trial. However, I intend to show that the abduction is pertinent to this case because Mr. Scott was abducted against his will, and that there was no intention on his part to flee with the property belonging to the Willis/Cooper advertising agency. In fact, I intend to show that prior to the time of his disappearance, Mr. Scott was on his way to deposit the funds in question into the company's corporate bank account. Throughout this case you will hear testimonies that are intended to support my client's claims. I ask that you keep an open mind when listening to these testimonies. If you do so, I believe that you will come to the conclusion that Mr. Scott's story not only cannot be dismissed as a fabrication, but it is very possible, if not most likely true."

Finch finished with his opening statement, walked back to his chair and sat next to Matt. The opening statements had been presented to the jury and it was time for the actual trial to begin.

The prosecution was first to act. The bailiff called Alan Cooper of the Willis/Cooper agency to the stand. Cooper was sworn in and Mr. Robbins began a line of questions intended to reveal the events of the day of Matt's disappearance.

"Mr. Cooper, how would you describe the defendant's demeanor at work on the day that he disappeared?"

"He seemed nervous," Cooper responded.

"Would you say nervous as though he had something to hide?"

Finch objected, claiming that Robbins was leading the witness. The judge agreed and sustained the objection. Robbins paused, and then re-phrased his question.

"Can you think of any reason that Mr. Scott may have had for his nervous appearance, and did you question him as to why he was acting in such a manner?"

"I believe that I asked if there was anything bothering him. He just said that he was going to see his doctor and he was concerned about the appointment. He didn't elaborate."

"Would you say that it was peculiar that he didn't offer any more explanation than that? After all, as I understand it, you were close friends who confided with one another on such matters weren't you?"

"Yes, we were, but I could see that he was agitated so I just let it go at that."

"Agitated you say. That sounds like a strange reaction to have just because of an appointment with a doctor."

"Objection," Finch shouted out. "The prosecution cannot predict how one might react under those circumstances."

"Sustained," ruled Judge Nathan.

Robbins continued, "Moving on to later in the day, he was leaving the office early, correct?"

"Yes, as I stated, he had an appointment with his physician, then he was going to make a deposit for me in our corporate bank account."

"Is it customary for employees to do the company banking?"

"No. We have an armored car service that takes care of that for us, but because of the presentation that we were making to a potential client, we missed the pickup that morning. Mr. Scott volunteered to make the deposit for me. He said he had personal business at the same institution that one holds our accounts, and he would be happy to make the deposit."

"What was the total amount of the deposit?"

"Some checks totaling $10,000 and $30,000 in cash."

"What was Mr. Scott's response when you revealed the amount of the deposit to him?"

"He said with that kind of money, along with his personal finances, that he would like to disappear and live in the tropics for a while. I took that as a joke."

"You say that you took Mr. Scott's reaction as a joke. Did he appear to have a humorous tone in his voice?"

"No, actually he seemed a very stoic, but I didn't pay it much attention."

"You stated that Mr. Scott mentioned personal finances along with the company's funds. Can you elaborate on that?"

"Yes. He also had a $5000 bonus that we had given him. I assumed that his reason for going to the bank was to deposit it."

"No further questions," Robbins said as he returned to his seat.

Finch rose and took the floor to cross examine Cooper.

"Mr. Cooper, you described my client as being nervous that day. Would you agree that he had cause to act in such a way, knowing that his physician was most likely going to advise him that he needed to have major surgery?"

"Yes," Cooper responded, then attempted to continue speaking. Finch, needing no further reply by Cooper, cut him off by interrupting him with, "yes or no will suffice."

"You stated that you had a close friendship with my client. Would it be fair to say that the two of you often joked around with one another at the office, and that Mr. Scott's comment about going to the tropics was not out of the ordinary?"

Cooper straightened up in his chair and glanced toward his attorney as he responded, "yes". Finch stepped back and declared no further questions. He was careful to extract only enough information from Cooper to diffuse any detrimental testimony that he may have given when questioned by Robbins.

The prosecution called James Ryan to the stand. He was one of the police detectives who recovered the briefcase that was taken from Matt's car.

"Detective Ryan, did you recover a briefcase that belonged to the defendant from a suspect in one of your robbery investigations?"

"Yes," Ryan replied.

"The police report states that the suspect in question admitted to taking the aforesaid brief case and its contents from the defendant's car on the day of his arrest. Correct?"

"Yes."

"Let the record show that it has been confirmed that, upon Mr. Scott's return, he was in possession of funds that were the property of the Willis/Cooper advertising agency, funds that he had taken and held in his possession for over one year."

Robbins finished questioning the detective and stepped back. Finch approached the bench and adjusted his glasses as he opened a document and began to question Ryan.

"Detective Ryan, your report disclosed the contents of the briefcase. I'm reading from that report, and it states that there were some checks and $10,000 in cash."

"Yes, that seems to be what I recall."

"Your report also stated that during your interrogation, the suspects in question admitted to spending approximately $20,000 of the cash contained in said briefcase. Is that true?"

"Yes," Ryan replied.

Finch stepped back and scratched his head as he removed his glasses, glimpsed at the jury, then turned his attention back to the detective.

"So when you recovered the briefcase, it contained approximately $10,000 in cash and the suspects in question admitted to spending approximately $20,000 of the money contained within the briefcase. That would mean that the briefcase contained approximately $30,000 when the suspects took it from Mr. Scott's car. Interesting; that's the same amount of money that Mr. Scott disappeared with over one year ago. It seems to me, that if Mr. Scott had intended on stealing the money, he would have spent at least some of it over the course of a whole year."

Robbins rose from his chair, "Objection, Conjecture! The defense cannot surmise what Mr. Scott would, or would not have done with the money."

"Sustained," agreed Judge Nathan.

"Moving on Detective Ryan. There's something that's been puzzling me. Mr. Scott was in possession of a company vehicle during his disappearance. The authorities checked the odometer against the trip reports that Mr. Scott was required to turn in to his office daily. How many miles had been traveled from the day of his disappearance, to the day he returned, according to those reports and the car's odometer?"

"Forty eight miles," Detective Ryan replied.

"That's interesting. I traveled the exact route that Mr. Scott drove from the office of Anderson/Cooper to his physician's office, then to his home. The mileage is exactly 48 miles. That would suggest to me that the vehicle never veered from its course, and yet during the police investigation into Mr. Scott's disappearance, the car was never found. It's like it just vanished from the face of the earth! How can that be?" he said as he threw his hands in the air and looked toward the jury with a look of amazement.

Finch turned his attention back to the Judge and declared no further questions. The bailiff called the next witness to the stand. It was John Thompson of the Thompson abduction and research Center. The prosecution's strategy would involve challenging Thompson as a credible witness. They realized that Matt's chances for an acquittal lie mostly with the jury believing that his abduction story was at least a possibility. Thompson took the stand and Robbins approached the bench.

"Mr. Thompson, as I understand it, your organization investigates stories of alien abductions. Is that correct?"

"Yes, we study claims of alien abduction and alien encounters and we are also involved in UFO research."

"For this case, let us concentrate on your abduction research. How many cases of abduction would you say that you have investigated?"

"I don't have an exact number, but I would approximate it to be in the neighborhood of two hundred."

"And of those two hundred, how many would you say offer concrete evidence that the abduction in question had actually occurred? Keep in mind, that when I use the phrase concrete evidence, I am referring to physical evidence that you would be able to present as proof that the claim of abduction was true."

"None... There has never been any physical evidence, but..."

Robbins quickly interrupted Thompson before he could elaborate. "Yes or no is sufficient. Mr. Thompson, would it be fair to say that many of the cases that you have investigated proved to be hoaxes?"

"Yes, it is to be expected that some claims would be erroneous."

"Would it also be fair to say, that because there is no proof to the contrary, that the remaining cases could also be considered as fraudulent?"

Finch interrupted, "objection, leading the witness."

"Sustained," replied Judge Nathan.

"No further questions," Robbins said as he stepped away from the bench. Finch approached the bench to cross examine Thompson.

"Approximately two hundred cases of abduction and encounters. That's quite a few. It would seem to be a frustrating task to continue to pursue these investigations without uncovering any evidence that an encounter may have ever occurred. Why would you keep investigating these claims?"

"Although I have no physical proof, I have seen indications that lead me to believe in the possibility that some of these abductions had taken place."

Robbins stood and made an objection claiming that Thompson's beliefs were not relevant. Finch countered, stating that Thompson's beliefs were the explanation for his continued investigation of UFO stories, and therefore were pertinent to Matt's defense. Judge Nathan agreed and overruled Robbins's objection. Finch instructed Thompson to continue.

"Throughout my interviews, I have found many similarities in the abduction cases that I've investigated."

Finch asked Thompson to elaborate. Thompson explained that throughout his investigations, he had found that a great number of abductees described their encounters so similarly, that he was hearing the same series of events repeatedly. He told of how the descriptions of the UFOs and the beings that inhabited them were consistent in detail. He explained that under hypnosis, abductees would give further details of their ordeals that were remarkably similar to one another.

"Mr. Thompson, you stated that hypnosis is used as a tool when conducting your interviews with abductees. Your colleague Mr. Robert Morrison, a clinical hypnotherapist, questioned Mr. Scott while in a hypnotic state. Please tell the court what Mr. Morrison's findings were during that session?"

"While under hypnosis, Mr. Scott gave a detailed description of two people that were also abducted. It wasn't until he was under hypnosis, that he remembered seeing these people during his encounter. He, in fact, would never have seen either of these people before his encounter, being that one is from India, the other from Great Britain. Neither one had ever been to the United States nor had Mr. Scott ever visited either of their home lands."

"Mr. Thompson, how did my client describe these two people?"

"He described one as a short, thin, dark complexioned man, with jet black hair and a beard, the other as a pale complexioned, heavyset woman with short, light brown hair and glasses."

Finch turned his attention to Judge Nathan.

"Your honor, if it pleases the court, I would like to introduce the two individuals that, while under hypnosis, my client identified during his interview with Mr. Thompson."

Finch walked over to where Raj Patel and Alice Harrison sat. He instructed them to stand and introduced them, then returned to the bench and resumed questioning Thompson.

"Mr. Thompson, I contacted you on June 23 of this year regarding my client's abduction. At that time you revealed to me that you had recently been in contact with two others, Raj Patel and Alice Harrison, who had claimed to have had the same experience as Matthew Scott. As is your practice, your colleague, Robert Morrison, put them under hypnosis and each one described two others. Alice Harrison saw Raj Patel and Matthew Scott. Raj Patel saw Alice Harrison and Matthew Scott. Each of the descriptions matched the person in question. Until under hypnosis, neither one remembered the other two. As you stated, they had never met before and yet under hypnosis, they not only gave a detailed description of one another, they also revealed the out of this world experience that all three had shared. I believe this supports the possibility that these three people may have actually experienced an alien encounter."

"Objection," Robbins called out. "The defense's statement is purely theoretical."

"Sustained," Judge Nathan said as he cautioned Finch not to theorize.

"Mr. Thompson I understand that in the last month, your agency has been contacted by numerous individuals who have had claims of alien encounters."

"Objection," Robbins called out. We are not here to debate other claims of alien encounters."

"Judge, if you'll permit me, I can show relevance," Finch explained.

"I'll allow it, but get to the point," Judge Nathan said sternly. "Continue Mr. Thompson," Finch said.

"Since Mr. Scott's case has generated so much publicity, others have come forth to share their experiences. My organization has been contacted by over sixty people who had been missing for over a year and returned to tell of their encounters, encounters very similar to those of Mr. Patel, Mrs. Harrison and Mr. Scott."

"You say sixty people to date have come forth with stories similar to Mr. Scott's story. Is it possible that because of the attention that Mr. Scott's story has received, these people may just be publicity seekers, and they're fabricating these stories?"

"No I don't believe so. The intricate details of Mr. Scott's story have not been released to the public, and yet each encounter is uncannily parallel to his. In each case it has been documented that the person in question had been missing for one year. The time period of all of the encounters, as well as the abduction dates and return dates, are all the same. They all had also believed that they were gone for only twenty four hours, even though a year had actually passed."

"How did they come to the conclusion that they had only been gone for twenty four hours?" Finch asked.

"Most of them wore wrist watches that displayed the time, as well as the date. Typically the watches revealed that only twenty four hours had gone by, and the date had advanced by only one day. That seemed to be the only indication of the time that had elapsed to any of these people. They had no idea as to how long they had actually been gone."

"Objection," Robbins called out."The defense is presenting hearsay evidence that was not presented at pretrial."

"Sustained," declared Judge Nathan. Finch stated no further questions and Thompson stepped down from the stand.

Finch asked that Raj Patel and Alice Harrison be called to the stand. Raj was first. Finch approached the bench. Finch's first question was to ask Raj if he was from India. He then asked if he had ever been to the United States before meeting with John Thompson. Raj answered yes he was from India and no he had never visited the United States.

Finch continued. "When did you first meet with John Thompson?"

"After reading about my abduction, Mr. Thompson contacted me and asked if I would be willing to come to his research center to discuss my encounter."

"And on what date did you arrive in the United States?"

"June 22," Raj replied.

"On that day Mr. Thompson's associate Robert Morrison put you under hypnosis and you described Alice Harrison and Matthew Scott. When did you actually meet Mr. Scott and Mrs. Harrison?"

"Mr. Thompson brought us together in his office on June 30th."

"So you gave an accurate description of the physical appearance of two people that you had never met, eight days prior to your first contact with them, correct?"

"Yes sir. I remembered seeing them during my abduction while under hypnosis."

"Mr. Patel you claim to have been abducted on June 21, 2009 and returned on June 21, 2010. Is that correct?"

"Yes," Raj replied.

"You also stated that when you first returned, you believed that you had only been gone for approximately twenty four hours. Can you elaborate?"

"It felt like only a short period of time that I was gone. When I returned, the date on my wrist watch indicated that only one day had passed."

"Please tell the court about your physical condition prior to your abduction."

Raj went on to reveal that he had fallen from a scaffold on a construction site, and as a result of the fall, he had fractures in both legs, a broken arm and a fractured skull.

"And when you returned from your encounter what was the status of your injuries?"

"I was completely healed. My physician could find no scar tissue to provide evidence that there were ever any broken bones."

"Thank you Mr. Patel, no further questions"

Robbins stood, but didn't approach the bench. He realized that if Raj Patel went into further detail on the recovery from his injuries, it could be detrimental to the prosecution's case. Robbins decided to make one observation before releasing Raj Patel from the witness stand.

"Mr. Patel, you stated that these injuries happened over a year ago. Is that correct?"

"Yes sir," Raj replied.

"I would like for the jury to note that one year is sufficient time for a fractured bone to heal. No further questions."

Alice Harrison was called to the stand next. Finch presented the same line of questions to her as he had presented to Raj Patel. Her testimony mirrored that of his. The abduction dates, as well as the twenty four hour time period that she had believed to be gone, matched the testimony of Raj Patel exactly. Finch questioned her about the cancer that was gone from her body upon her return. Unlike Raj Patel whose injuries could have eventually healed, as Robbins pointed out to the court, Alice's cancer was terminal. She testified and presented medical records to prove that she was cancer free. Finch finished his questions for Alice Harrison and Robbins approached the bench.

"Mrs. Harrison, were you under medical treatment for your cancer?"

"Yes."

"Please explain the extent of those treatments to the court."

"I was undergoing standard radiation treatments until about a month before my abduction. At that time I started a new more concentrated and aggressive form of radiation therapy because of the advanced stage of my cancer."

"Your records indicate that you were terminal. Did the prognosis change with this new course of action?"

"I was informed that this new procedure was more successful in laboratory tests, but there was no proof that it would be more successful than conventional radiation treatments."

Robbins backed away from the witness stand, retrieved a document from his briefcase and returned to address the judge.

" Your honor, let the record show that I am providing documentation that reveals this new procedure that Mrs. Harrison is talking about has been practiced for over a year, and has had much more success treating cancer patients than previous treatments have had. In fact many patients diagnosed as terminal, previous to this new form of radiation therapy, have gone into full remission after receiving the new form of treatment. It is very possible that Mrs. Harrison could have had a full recovery from her illness because of these treatments. Mrs. Harrison may have recovered from her disease, not from some out of this world alien technology, but from modern science developed in our own laboratories."

"Objection," Finch called out, "counselor is to be obtaining testimony at this time, not theorizing on Mrs. Harrison's recovery."

"Overruled, prosecution has presented documentation to support the argument. Continue counselor," said Judge Nathan. Robbins finished his questions for Alice Harrison. It was Matt's turn to take the stand. Finch was first to question him.

"Mr. Scott, you have heard Mr. Patel and Mrs. Harrison's accounts of their abductions. How similar to their experiences would you say your encounter was?"

"Objection," said Robbins." The defense's line of questions indicates that Mr. Scott had not heard the testimony of Mr. Patel and Mrs. Harrison until now, when in fact the three of them had discussed their alleged encounters previous to their appearance in the courtroom today. It is very possible that they could have coordinated their stories to sound similar. Counsel is clearly misleading the jury."

"Sustained," ruled Judge Nathan. Finch continued.

"I'll rephrase that Mr. Scott. We have heard Mr. Patel and Mrs. Harrison's accounts of their encounters while under hypnosis. While under hypnosis you also revealed the details of your encounter. Do you remember those details?"

"I remember some. Mr. Thompson filled me in on the rest."

"And how similar would you say that the three accounts given under hypnosis were to one another?"

"Objection," Robbins cried out as he raised his hands in disgust. "Counselor is still attempting to mislead the jury."

Finch responded, "Your Honor, the interviews that were conducted under hypnosis were done separately. Mr. Patel, Mrs. Harrison and my client simply could not have known what one another would say while under hypnosis."

"Overruled," said the judge.

"Continue Mr. Scott," Finch said.

"They were more than similar. I experienced the same exact things as they did."

"When you say the exact same things, what do you mean?"

"When the abduction first began to happen, the bright sunny sky turned dark abruptly. Suddenly the sky seemed to open up and I saw a blinding light. My car shook violently for a few seconds, and then a tranquil feeling came over me as I passed out. I awoke seemingly to be floating on air. I could see the aliens all around me and I could see Mr. Patel and Mrs. Harrison. Off in the distance, I saw other people levitating above the surface but they were too far a way to make out any distinguishing features. What seemed like a short time later, I woke up in my car on the side of the road?"

Finch declared no further questions. Robbins approached the bench.

"Mr. Scott, have you ever seen the old television program, the Twilight Zone?"

"Yes," Matt replied.

"Yes, I thought so. Most everyone has. It's on television in reruns all the time. The themes for the twilight zone episodes are always based on science fiction, many of the episodes having to do with aliens and UFOs."

"Objection," Finch called out. "A fictional TV show has no relevance to this case."

"Actually it does your honor," countered Robbins. "If the court will extend the same courtesy to me to make a point, as it did to the defense, I will show relevancy."

"Overruled," I'll allow it, but you're on a short leash counselor," barked Judge Nathan.

Robbins retreated to the prosecution table, and then returned with a manila folder. He opened it and removed its contents.

"Mr. Scott, I would like to read part of the script from Twilight Zone episode 35 that first aired in 1965. The title is, Vanished from Earth. It reads, and I quote. *I stood in awe of the bright light as it lit up the dark sky. The ground shook and I was consumed by the blinding light as I fell into a deep sleep.* End quote. That sounds remarkably similar to your story, and in turn, to the stories of Mr. Patel and Mrs. Harrison wouldn't you say?"

Matt responded uneasily. "Yes...but"

Robbins interrupted. "That suggests to me that maybe your story lacks originality. In fact, maybe your story is just as fictional as the twilight zone episode. Could it be that's where you came up with this incredible tale that you're presenting as fact in the courtroom here today?"

"Objection," Finch blurted out. The prosecution is attempting to claim that just because a fictional story has some similarities to this case, that my client's story must also be fictional."

"Sustained," said Judge Nathan. Robbins continued.

"Mr. Scott your story of aliens and UFOs is very entertaining to say the least, but let's talk about the day that you left the office of the Willis/ Cooper advertising agency a year ago. There are some things that I find quite puzzling. It is difficult for me to understand why, when you left your office on the day of your disappearance, that you chose to go to see your doctor before conducting business at the bank. After all, the bank was only a few blocks away from the doctor's office. Wouldn't you have been more comfortable making that deposit beforehand, rather than carrying that large sum of money around?"

"I guess I was just in a hurry to see my doctor. I was eager to get the results of my MRI and to find out what course of action the surgeon was going to recommend."

Robbins paused. "I was under the impression that the doctor had already informed you that you needed surgery. Isn't that true?"

"Yes, I just didn't know yet how extensive that the surgery was going to be."

"I guess I can see why you were so anxious to make your appointment, and yet you testified that on the way to your doctor's office, you stopped to buy a loaf of bread. What made you think that you could take the time to stop to buy a loaf of bread, but not stop at the bank to deposit a large sum of money? That seems very strange to me."

Matt could not come up with an answer to Robbins question. His mind went blank as he tried to rationalize his actions. Robbins knew that the jury would consider it a sign of weakness if Matt didn't answer the question so he continued on before Matt could respond.

" Mr. Scott, you not only did not stop to make the bank deposit before your appointment, you also failed to stop to make a deposit after leaving the doctor's office that day. In fact, you never did make the deposit. You testified that your alleged abduction had taken place on a rural road halfway between your office and your home. I ask you again. Why were you still in possession of those funds at that time? Why didn't you make the deposit after you left your doctor's office? The funds belonging to the Willis/Cooper advertising agency never were deposited. Those funds were in your possession from that day until a year later when you were arrested by the police as you returned home with an incredible tale of being abducted by aliens. I contend that once you were taken into custody, you came up with this wild story in an absurd attempt to explain your disappearance. I believe it never was your intention to deposit the company funds into their corporate account."

Robbins swiftly moved away from the bench as he declared, "no further questions." He did not want a response from Matt. It would be more detrimental to Matt's testimony to leave the jury with the thought that Matt may not have intended to make the deposit of the company funds as he was entrusted to do by Alan Cooper. Dr. Rayford was next to take the stand. Finch approached the bench.

"Dr. Rayford, would you please describe the physical condition of Mr. Scott when you last saw him a year ago?"

"He was in very poor physical condition. His mobility was severely compromised because of the condition of his spine. The L1, L2 and L3 vertebrae were out of alignment. The discs were worn, causing pressure on his sciatic nerve. This caused pain to travel into his legs, throwing him off balance. He also had arthritis in both hips and knees."

"And what was your recommendation at that time?"

"He needed surgery to align his spine and take pressure off the sciatic nerve."

"Would this surgery allow Mr. Scott to move about like any normal healthy person?"

"Unfortunately there was so much deterioration in the vertebrae and discs, that even if his spine was surgically repaired, his mobility would still be severely compromised. The main objective of the surgery would have been to relieve the pressure on the nerve and alleviate his pain."

"You examined Mr. Scott after his return and you studied the results of his latest MRI. What was your reaction to Mr. Scott's recovery?"

"I was astonished. The MRI showed no sign of any deterioration in the vertebrae or discs. His spine is perfectly aligned and there is no sign of arthritis in his hips or knees. What's even more amazing is that I could find no indication that a medical procedure of any kind was ever performed on Mr. Scott."

"And how did you come to that conclusion?"

"There are no scars on his body. If he had been operated on there would be scars where the incisions were made, and there would also be scar tissue on the mended bone."

"Even one year later?"

"Yes," Dr. Rayford confirmed.

"Dr. Rayford when Mr. Scott disappeared a year ago, his hair was turning gray. He had a receding hairline and a bald spot on the top of his head. When he returned, he had a full head of thick dark hair. You examined his scalp. Do you have an explanation for the re-growth of his hair?"

"Objection," Robbins howled out. "Counselor is wasting the court's time with a line of questions that are irrelevant to the case."

"Your Honor, the condition of my client's scalp is relevant to his claim of abduction, which in turn is relevant to the pending charges against him."

"Objection overruled. Counsel for the prosecution and counsel for the defense please approach the bench for a sidebar."

Finch and Robbins stepped up to the bench. Judge Nathan lowered his voice and then sternly directed his words toward Finch.

"Mr. Finch, I will allow you to continue, but be cautioned to quickly establish a connection between your line of questions and this case."

"Yes your honor," Finch said as he and Robbins stepped back. Finch continued.

"Dr. Rayford, after examining Mr. Scott's scalp, were you able to come up with an explanation for the re-growth of his hair, as well as the change in color?"

"No. There is no evidence of any type of hair transplant to account for the re-growth. What I find most curious though, is that the hair follicles were dark. His hair had turned gray. Even if he had dyed his hair, the roots would not have changed from the gray color that occurs naturally with the ageing process."

"Getting back to Mr. Scott's physical condition, you removed a mole from Mr. Scott's neck one year ago. Is that correct?"

"Yes," replied Dr. Rayford.

"As I understand it, the procedure to remove that mole left a scar on his neck. That scar should have healed, then faded away within two to three weeks of the procedure, leaving no mark as evidence that the scar had ever been there. Is that correct?"

"Yes it is."

"I have a picture taken of Mr. Scott's neck four days after his return, which happened to be over a year after you performed the procedure to remove the mole from his neck. Can you explain why the scar still appears on Mr. Scott's neck, one year after you performed that procedure?"

"No, from the stage that the healing process is in, I would say that the procedure had been done no more than seven days prior to this picture being taken."

"No further questions Your Honor," Finch said as he returned to his seat. Robbins approached the bench.

"Dr. Rayford, can you assure the court that you are 100% positive that Mr. Scott would not have the mobility that he has today if he opted for an alternative treatment, such as acupuncture or chiropractic?"

"No, not 100% but..."

Robbins interrupted. "Yes or no is sufficient. No further questions Your Honor," he said as he promptly returned to his seat.

Dr. Rayford was the last witness to be called. Before the attorneys presented their closing arguments, Judge Nathan asked if there were any exhibits to be brought in front of the court. Finch rose and approached the bench.

"Yes your honor. I would like to present five exhibits."

The bailiff collected the exhibits and handed them to Judge Nathan. Finch explained the contents of each exhibit as the judge carefully examined them.

"Exhibit A is a picture taken of a scar on Mr. Scott's neck. Dr. Rayford testified that this scar is from the mole that he removed from Mr. Scott's neck one year ago. He also testified that the scar should have healed; leaving no visible trace that it was removed, within two to three weeks of the procedure to remove it. Exhibit B is an affidavit from Orion Laboratory verifying that the loaf of bread that Mr. Scott bought over a year ago was tested, and it was proven that it had never been frozen or preserved in any way. If that loaf of bread was a year old, as the expiration date indicates, it would have molded and turned stale. In fact, that loaf of bread had to be at least six months old, being that this particular variety of bread hasn't been produced in over six months. This affidavit shows that tests indicate the bread is not only fresh; it appeared to be only three to four days old at the time these tests were performed. Exhibit C contains sixty affidavits from individuals who, over the past two weeks, have been interviewed by John Thompson, of the Thompson research center. The circumstances of each and every case mirror those of Raj Patel, Alice Harrison and Matthew Scott. These affidavits contain sworn testimony from physicians, confirming that each individual had a life altering experience in the time period that they were missing. That time period is consistent with the date of disappearance and the date of return of Matthew Scott, Alice Harrison, and Raj Patel. Exhibits D and E contain affidavits from the physicians who treated Alice Harrison and Raj Patel. These exhibits document their physical condition, prior to, and subsequent to their yearlong disappearance. The affidavits contained herein state that there is no logical explanation for the physical metamorphosis that has taken place in the physical being of Mrs. Harrison and Mr. Patel"

Judge Nathan took the exhibits into his possession and studied each document and picture before querying the jury to confirm that they understood the significance of the exhibits. Satisfied with their response, he summoned the attorneys for their closing arguments. Robbins was first to address the jury.

"Ladies and gentlemen of the jury; first of all, I would like to thank you for taking the time to be here today. You have heard testimony meant to support the defendant's claim that he was abducted by aliens. In fact most of the testimony that you have heard today has pertained to that claim. I hope that you haven't been distracted by these incredible stories. You must remember that Mr. Scott is on trial, not for his claim of an alien encounter, but for the crime of embezzlement and grand theft. Whether or not his story is true, the fact is that he left the office of Willis/Cooper with property and cash in his possession that belonged to the company. They, in good faith, trusted Mr. Scott to deposit those funds in the company bank account on his way to an appointment with his physician. I want you to keep in mind that the bank was on the way to his appointment, and yet you heard the defense testify that he did not stop at the bank first. In fact you heard the defendant admit that he not only did not stop to make the deposit on the way to his doctor appointment, he failed to go back to the bank after leaving the doctor's office. He testified that because his mind was preoccupied with his doctor appointment, he forgot to make the bank deposit, and yet he could remember to stop and buy a loaf of bread. A year after his disappearance Mr. Scott resurfaced. He told you that he returned to the house that he had resided in with his wife and child. It was there that the police were called and Mr. Scott was taken into custody. He stated that a brief case containing the missing funds was in his car and, that while in police custody, said funds were stolen from his car. You heard Officer Ryan attest to the fact that this was true, and the suspects had been apprehended. You also heard that the suspects admitted to the theft. You must understand that the suspects who took the money from Mr. Scott are not on trial. Mr. Scott had those funds in his possession illegally for over a year after taking them from the Willis/Cooper Agency. That those funds were stolen from him only goes to prove that fact. Ladies and gentlemen of the jury this is a clear cut case. The defendant took funds that didn't belong to him. He vanished and was apprehended a year later with said funds in his possession. I would expect that you have no choice but to find the defendant guilty. Thank you."

Robbins took his seat. Finch took a deep breath and buttoned his suit jacket as he stood to address the jury.

"Ladies and gentlemen of the jury, I also would like to thank you for your time today. The prosecution has reminded you of what you heard today. I too want to remind you of what you heard, and also of what you saw. Two people are in the courtroom today that have shared an experience with Mr. Scott. You heard from Alice Harrison. She told you that a year ago she had terminal cancer. Her doctors used the most aggressive radiation therapy available at that time to no avail. They concluded that, at best, she had six months to live, and yet she stands before you today, cancer free. Medical science as we know it has no explanation for her miraculous recovery. Raj Patel testified that he fell from a scaffold at a construction site. Doctors told him that his injuries would leave him crippled for life. As with Mrs. Harrison, there is no medical explanation for his recovery. My client, Mr. Scott, was in need of major back surgery to correct a disabling condition that was worsening with every passing day. In fact you heard Dr. Rayford testify that, without the surgery, he would most certainly end up confined to a wheelchair. Dr. Rayford also told you that he could not explain Mr. Scott's miraculous recovery. He testified that there were no signs of any medical procedure ever being performed on Mr. Scott. You saw affidavits from the physicians who treated Alice Harrison and Raj Patel, confirming that there was no evidence of medical procedures performed on their patients, and no explanation for their miraculous recoveries. Look at these individuals. They are in just as good condition, and just as healthy as you or I. Throughout this trial, the time period That Mrs. Harrison, Mr. Patel and my client had believed that they were gone has been brought to your attention. To them, what was actually a year, seemed like only hours. I have no explanation for that. Is it possible that time was somehow altered during their encounters? Exhibits A and B would seem to support that theory. You saw in exhibit A that, as confirmed by Dr. Rayford, a scar on Mr. Scott's neck that should have been completely healed over a year ago seemed to be only weeks into the healing process. In exhibit B, a one year-old loaf of bread that was in Mr. Scott's possession during his encounter was still fresh. After all you have seen and heard today, you must consider the possibility of some out of this world intervention. I would like to share something with you that I came across while doing research for this trial. It is a quote by the respected rocket scientist and engineer, Wemher Von Braun. He was a leading figure in the development of rocket technology in the United States and Germany during and after World War Two, and also was regarded as the preeminent rocket engineer of the twentieth century in his role with NASA. I quote. *"Our sun is one of one hundred billion stars in our galaxy. Our galaxy is one of billions of galaxies populating the universe. It would be the height of presumption to think that we are the only living thing in that enormous immensity."* End quote. I have also learned, while preparing for this trial, that even the Catholic Church recognizes the fact that we may not be alone in this universe. We have traveled into outer space and landed on the moon. Who's to say that there are not others out there with far more advanced technology in space travel as well as medical procedures? Is it possible that they have visited our world? To be honest with you, I would have scoffed at that idea before I met Mr. Scott. I now believe that the evidence proves that we are not alone. The prosecution has reminded you that this case is not about alien abduction. The prosecution is right. This case is about whether my client, Mr. Scott, intentionally embezzled funds from his company, the key word being intentionally. Although this case is about only that charge, the abduction claim of Mr. Scott is pertinent to whether he willingly and intentionally disappeared with the funds in question. You heard Mr. Scott testify that he was a little out of sorts that day. He was anxious about the meeting with Dr. Rayford. He admitted that he didn't go to the bank before his appointment or after the appointment. Instead of taking the time to go back to the bank near his office, his intention was to make the deposit at the branch close to his home. He told you of the abduction that took place on the rural road halfway between his employer's office and his home, thus keeping him from reaching his destination. For this reason he was unable to make the deposit as planned on that day. Ladies and gentlemen of the jury, after the testimonies that you have heard today and the evidence that you have seen, you must consider that my client's claim of abduction is very much a possibility, and there is reasonable doubt that it was ever his intention to commit a crime. I ask that you find my client, Matthew Scott, not guilty. Thank you."

Finch took his seat and Judge Nathan, as is routine in jury trials, offered the prosecution the opportunity to make a closing rebuttal.

Robbins stood as he replied, "yes Your Honor," and then turned to face the jury.

"Ladies and gentlemen of the jury, I can't stress this enough, so I will remind you one more time. You have heard an overwhelming amount of information about UFO theories and Mr. Scott's alleged alien abduction. You must remember that we are here today to determine if he is guilty of a crime, not whether or not he experienced an alien encounter. Once again, the defendant took money that didn't belong to him. He had it in his possession for one whole year until he was apprehended by the authorities. The evidence shows that the defendant, Matthew Scott, is guilty of the crime that he is accused of in this court today. Thank you."

The verdict was now in the hands of the jury. Judge Nathan addressed the jurors with final instructions before they retired to the seclusion of the deliberation room.

"Members of the jury, this trial is about whether or not the crimes of embezzlement and grand theft have been committed. The simple definition of embezzlement is to steal money and or property entrusted into one's care. A person convicted of this crime will be sentenced as determined by the court. You are only to consider the evidence brought forth today in the form of sworn testimony and exhibits. You are to understand that the attorney's arguments may not be considered as evidence. They are only meant to help you understand the events leading up to the trial. You must consider the defendant innocent until proven guilty."

Judge Nathan finished his instructions to the jury. The bailiff called out, "all rise," and the jury filed out of the court room to determine the verdict. Finch rose and led Matt into the hall outside of the courtroom where they were joined by Amy, Alice Harrison, Raj Patel and John Thompson. Amy took Matt's hand and did her best to be supportive and provide a positive attitude. Matt's tone was nervous as he questioned Finch.

"So what do you think Thomas?"

Finch could sense the tension in Matt's voice. He didn't want to mislead Matt into thinking they had won the case, and yet he wanted to appear positive.

"I think that everything went as well as we could have hoped for. I paid close attention to the demeanor of the jury throughout the trial. Their body language seemed to indicate that they were receptive to the facts that were presented to support the idea of your abduction as a possibility."

"That's good?" Matt replied.

"That's very good. If they accept that possibility, then we have reasonable doubt that you intended to commit a crime. That's where your chances of an acquittal lie. We've presented a lot of strong evidence on your behalf Matt. All we can do now is sit back and wait for the jury's decision."

Finch's words helped Matt feel a little more at ease as he sat with Amy on one of the benches outside of the courtroom and waited for word on the jury's verdict.

The jury sat together at a large oval table in the deliberation room as they discussed the case. They agreed that the alien abduction story seemed farfetched at first, however as the trial progressed, the defense presented some very convincing arguments in Matt's favor. The unexplainable circumstances such as the one year-old loaf of bread that was still fresh, the wristwatches that had only advanced one day in time over the past year, and the miraculous physical recoveries that Alice, Raj and Matt had experienced, made it impossible for them to dismiss the abduction defense from consideration. One of the jurors brought up the point that over and over, throughout the trial, they were reminded that the case was not about Matt's claim of abduction. He was on trial for embezzlement and grand theft only, not whether or not he was abducted by aliens. The jury members were split on how much weight the abduction theory should factor into their decision. Another juror brought up the question of Matt's decision of when to make a bank deposit. He recalled that Matt didn't make the deposit before going to meet with his physician as planned, nor did he make the deposit promptly after leaving that appointment. The question of why he would carry that much money with him as he traveled to a branch of the bank fifteen miles away instead of going back to the much closer branch was a puzzling one.

One of the jurors paced back and forth, then stopped and addressed the group.

"Why would he return after a whole year with all the money still in his possession? His lawyer pointed that out to us. Like his lawyer said, it's strange that Mr. Scott wouldn't have spent at least some of the money if it was his intention to steel it in the first place."

Another juror brought up the whereabouts of Matt's car.

"Why didn't the authorities find the missing car? The mileage on the odometer indicated that the car had only been driven the exact distance from Mr. Scott's office to his home. Don't you think the police should have found it abandoned somewhere along that route. I don't know about the rest of you, but I find that to be very strange…kind of creeps me out. I mean, how do you explain that?"

The jurors went back and forth on how much the abduction theory should affect their decision. Whether or not Matt had intended on making the deposit was further questioned when another juror reminded the group that Matt had told his boss, that with the money he was to deposit, and his personal finances, he would like to disappear and live in the tropics. They had to decide whether Matt had intended for this statement to be a joke, as the defense claimed, or if it was actually a statement of intention as the prosecuting attorney implied. The jury foreman rose from his chair.

"Looks like we're gonna be here for a while," he said as he stretched the kinks from his arms and legs.

When the trial began the jurors expected to be arriving at a quick decision, but now they realized that this case was much more complicated than it seemed at the beginning. Each jury member had reservations about voting guilty or not guilty as they reviewed the case from the attorney's opening statements to the closing arguments. They continued to deliberate, some jurors leaning toward accepting the abduction as a defense, while others felt they should disregard it altogether. It became clear that the verdict would hinge on that decision.

Finally one of the jurors suggested a course of action that would ultimately decide the verdict. First they would review the case from beginning to end, accepting the evidence that was brought forth to support Matt's alien abduction claim. They would then review the case from beginning to end again, this time ignoring the abduction theory altogether, and looking only at evidence not linked to the abduction story. The members of the jury all agreed on this course of action and proceeded to study the case from each angle. After considering both scenarios they would be ready to render their decision.

Chapter 24

MATT AND HIS ENTOURAGE CONSISTING of Amy, Thomas Finch, John Thompson, Raj Patel and Alice Harrison sat huddled outside the courtroom awaiting the jury's decision. It had been nearly five hours since the jury seceded to the deliberation room to decide Matt's fate. Matt glanced at his watch as he nervously questioned Finch about the amount of time that the jury was out.

"I believe that it's a good sign that the jury has been out for this long Matt. If they weren't even considering the abduction in their decision, they would have returned rather quickly, probably with a guilty verdict. Remember, even though the case is not about your abduction, it hinges on whether or not they accept the abduction as a possibility. I don't like to speculate, but my guess is that we've convinced them to take a good hard look at the evidence that we've presented to them today. If they're doing that, then we've won half the battle."

Finch gave Matt a reassuring pat on the back, and then rose to his feet.

"I'm going in to see if I can get a feel for what's going on in there," he said as he walked into the courtroom.

Matt rose from his seat as he watched the large wooden doors close behind Finch. He leaned against the hallway wall and stared down at the floor as he waited for Finch to reappear with word on the jury's return. Amy walked over and put her arm around his waist as she whispered words of encouragement. "It won't be long now," she said as she kissed him on the cheek, then rested her head on his shoulder.

John Thompson, Raj Patel, and Alice Harrison stood and gathered around Matt and Amy. All were quiet in the hall now as they waited for Finch to reappear. A short time passed and Finch emerged from the courtroom. "They're ready," he announced. Matt's heart pounded with the realization that he was about to learn of the jury's decision. Matt entered the courtroom and he and Finch walked side-by-side to the defense table. Amy and the others took their seats in the courtroom. The bailiff called out, "all rise," as the judge entered the courtroom and seated himself at the bench. The jury filed in one by one, took their seats in the juror's box, and the court room was seated. Judge Nathan addressed the jury, asking if they had reached a verdict. The foreman answered, "Yes Your Honor," and the judge turned his attention toward Matt.

"Will the defendant rise," he instructed. He then turned to the jury foreman and requested the decision.

"On the count of embezzlement, what say you?"

"Not guilty," replied the foreman.

The courtroom was crowded with spectators and reporters who had gathered to witness the bizarre case that was presented in the court on this day. A murmur from the gallery circulated around the courtroom as the decision was announced. Judge Nathan announced, "order in the court," and continued to question the jury foreman.

"On the count of grand theft auto, what say you?"

"Not guilty," the foreman replied again, and again the court room was abuzz.

Judge Nathan requested quiet, and then turned his attention to Matt.

"This court finds the defendant, Matthew Scott, not guilty on all charges. Mr. Scott you are free to go."

Matt stood dumbfounded. He almost couldn't believe that he heard the words, "You're free to go". The momentary shock that he felt faded as Finch turned to him and shook his hand vigorously as he reiterated the jury's decision." You're free Matt." Amy hurriedly approached Matt and threw her arms around him. John Thompson, Raj Patel and Alice Harrison joined Matt, Amy and Finch in a celebratory group hug. Matt looked across the courtroom to see Alan Cooper and his lawyer preparing to exit the room. He had hoped that, if the decision went in his favor, he could renew his friendship with Cooper. It was apparent however that wasn't going to be the case as Cooper scornfully looked back at Matt while exiting the courtroom. Although Matt was elated with the jury's decision, he was saddened by the thought of the loss of a good friend. He turned his attention back to Finch who was packing his briefcase with notes from the trial.

"So what happens now Thomas? Where does Willis/Cooper go from here?"

"Now that you've been acquitted, it'll be deemed that you intended to deposit the company's funds as planned. Any charges pertaining to those funds will now be brought against the men who stole the briefcase from your car."

Finch gathered his notes, slipped them into his briefcase and proceeded to lead Matt out of the courtroom.

"Congratulation's Matt, looks like we can chalk one up for the judicial system."

"Matt smiled at Finch as he let out a sigh of relief, "thank God Thomas. I've got to admit, as happy as I am that the decision went my way, I had my doubts. I wanna pinch myself to see if I'm dreaming, but I don't dare."

"Go ahead Matt. Pinch yourself all you want. You're definitely not dreaming," Finch said as he patted Matt on the back.

"So what do you think made the jury decide in my favor?" Matt asked curiously.

"It's hard to say Matt. You never know what goes through juror's minds when they're deciding a verdict. If I had to guess I would say that they came to the conclusion that your abduction was a real possibility.

Just the idea that your story could be true brings reasonable doubt that you intended to commit a crime. Like I told you before, getting the jury to accept the possibility of the abduction was half the battle."

As Matt and Finch were making their way out of the courtroom John Thompson approached them.

"Matt, I'd like you to meet a colleague of mine. This is George Armstrong."

Matt paused and shook Mr. Armstrong's hand as Thompson continued on.

"Mr. Armstrong is a journalist and novelist. He's written many articles on the work that we've been doing at the research center. He... Well I'll let him tell you the rest."

"Mr. Scott, as John has told you, I'm a writer. I've been following your case ever since I heard it mentioned on the evening news. John has filled me in on the details of your encounter, as well as the encounters of Mrs. Harrison and Mr. Patel and the many others. It's a fascinating story and I'd like to write about it. I should say I'd like to collaborate with you on a book deal."

Matt was at a loss for words. He had never thought about something like a book coming from his experience. His mind had been occupied only with thoughts of making it through the trial and being exonerated of the charges against him. He looked at Amy, then back at Armstrong.

"I really want to put this all behind me. I'll have to think about it."

"I understand Matt. I realize that you've been through a lot. I'm not looking for a commitment from you right now. Take some time to mull it over. We can talk later if you're interested."

Armstrong pulled a business card from his wallet and handed it to Matt. He told him that he would be in contact after Matt had some time to unwind from the hectic events of the trial. Armstrong and Matt shook hands and Armstrong left the courtroom. Matt and the others proceeded to exit the building. Thompson stopped Matt one more time before they reached the doors leading out of the courthouse.

"Matt there's one more thing that I want to prepare you for."

"What's that?" Matt said as he put his hand on the courthouse door.

"When you walk out that door there are going to be a group of reporters shoving microphones in your face. I suggest that for the time being, all you should say is no comment. They're going to try and twist your words around to sensationalize their stories. I think it's to your advantage to only do interviews on a one on one basis that you've prepared for by previewing the questions that are going to be asked. I suggest that you consult with Finch and I before you agree to any interviews. If you decide to do the book deal, you don't want the press, or even worse, those tabloid rags misquoting anything you might say."

"I got it. Thanks John," Matt replied.

Finch opened the courthouse door and they exited the building. They walked out onto the steps leading away from the courthouse and as Thompson had predicted, reporters were there to snap pictures and shout out questions to Matt. Finch and Thompson were able to fend off the reporters while Matt and Amy hurried to their car. Matt could hear the barrage of questions being tossed his way as he and Amy made their way to the car. Questions like, "Mr. Scott do you feel like you beat the system by claiming to be abducted?" and "Couldn't you have been more original with your description of the aliens?" It was clear that most of the questions that were being fired at him were meant to discredit his story. Matt and Amy quickly entered their car and exited the parking lot. Matt watched as the reporters disappeared in the rearview mirror. The reporter's questions brought forth the realization that the jury had accepted his abduction as a possibility not as a matter of fact. How would people look at him now? He thought. Would he become a laughingstock, and of more concern, would he be able to find another job to support his family? It was clear now that he would have to collaborate with George Armstrong on the book deal, if for nothing other than a source of income.

Amy observed Matt as they drove off. She expected to see him display an expression of elation, but instead noticed a look of concern.

"I expected you to be happy with the outcome of the trial. Is something bothering you?"

"I guess I'm just wondering how people are going to react to me now. You heard those reporters. They just as much called me a liar with those questions."

"Matt we can't worry about what other people think. We know the truth. You presented your case in court, what else can you do?"

"I think I'm going to go ahead and work with Armstrong on the book. If I can get my story out there, and Armstrong can make it believable, then maybe people will be more willing to accept the possibility that it really happened."

Amy and Matt continued on home. They turned off the highway and onto the rural road that led home. He approached the spot where his abduction occurred and pulled to the side of the road.

"Why are we stopping?" Amy asked.

"This is the spot where they took me."

"Oh my God, I didn't even think that we would be passing by here. How's it feel to be here again?"

"I thought that it would feel creepy or scary, something like that, but I really don't feel anything. Come on, let's get out. I want to look around."

Amy hesitantly followed Matt as he exited the car. Matt may not have felt any emotions but Amy was nervous about visiting the spot where her husband had vanished over a year ago. She held on to Matt's arm as he carefully surveyed the area looking for signs that the aliens had been there. He stopped abruptly as he noticed the faded remains of the unexplained imprints that Thompson had believed to have been left by the alien craft.

"This is it, this is the spot," he said as he pointed to the ground. "I guess the weather has eroded away most of the markings."

Amy tugged on his arm and gently pulled him back to the car.

"Maybe you don't feel anything, but I've got a chill going through my body. Let's get out of here before they come back. I don't want to lose you again."

Matt laughed and gave her a hug as they walked toward the car. "Okay, let's go home."

Chapter 25

MATT AND AMY PULLED INTO their driveway and exited the car. Jason saw them and ran from the front porch to greet his mom and dad. Kathy stood at the top of the steps watching as Jason jumped into his dad's waiting arms

"Congratulations Matt. I wish I could have been there, "Kathy said, while embracing Matt and Amy as they reached the top of the stairs. "I'll bet you two are starving. Dinner will be ready soon."

"I'll help Kathy in the kitchen. Why don't you and Jason play one of his computer games while we're getting dinner ready," Amy said as she followed Kathy into the kitchen.

Matt grabbed Jason by the arm and playfully wrestled him to the floor.

"Do you wanna play one of your games buddy?"

Jason nodded yes in answer to Matt's question and ran to get one of his video games. Matt turned the video player on and took the game cartridge from Jason.

"What game have you got there pal?" He asked Jason.

"Spacemen," Jason yelled out.

Matt read the title of the game to himself, "Attack of the Space Invaders." He shook his head, then tossed the game onto the coffee table and turned to Jason.

"Hey buddy. I've got a better idea. Let's go out and throw the ball around in the backyard. What do you say?"

Jason jumped up, grabbed his baseball and glove, and ran through the kitchen and out the back door. Matt jogged close behind him and as he passed by Amy he said, "We're gonna throw the ball around. Call us when dinner is ready."

"I thought that you were going to play a video game." Amy said.

Matt looked back at Amy as he chased Jason out the door.

"I think I've played that game enough for one lifetime," he said as the screen door slammed shut behind him.